September 2021

Valley Cottage Library
110 Route 303
Valley Cottage, NY
10989

www.vclib.org

THE HIDDENSEEK

NATE CERNOSEK

G. P. PUTNAM'S SONS

G. P. PUTNAM'S SONS
An imprint of Penguin Random House LLC, New York

alloy**entertainment**

Produced by Alloy Entertainment
30 Hudson Yards, 22nd Floor
New York, NY 10001

Visit us online at penguinrandomhouse.com

Library of Congress Cataloging-in-Publication Data
Names: Cernosek, Nate, author.
Title: The Hiddenseek / Nate Cernosek.
Description: New York: G. P. Putnam's Sons, [2021] | Summary: "A brother and sister
are transported to a strange world based on the game hide-and-seek, where they
are pursued by a cursed witch"—Provided by publisher.
Identifiers: LCCN 2021006126 | ISBN 9781984816764 (hardcover) |
ISBN 9781984816771 (epub)
Subjects: CYAC: Hide-and-seek—Fiction. | Brothers and sisters—Fiction. | Witches—Fiction. |
Memory—Fiction.
Classification: LCC PZ7.1.C46495 Hi 2021 | DDC [Fic]—dc23
LC record available at https://lccn.loc.gov/2021006126

Printed in the United States of America
ISBN 9781984816764

1 3 5 7 9 10 8 6 4 2

SKY

Design by Marikka Tamura | Text set in Italian Old Style MT Std

For Lucia and Tommy

1

THE SUN HUNG LOW IN THE SKY, SINKING TOWARD THE HORIZON. A slight breeze stirred the trees and blew through the empty swings. Their chains jostled and clinked. The jungle gym was deserted, as were the monkey bars, the seesaw, the slides. The park was empty.

Almost.

There was one child still at the park. One child who had been left behind.

Her name was Holly Thorn. She was playing hide-and-seek.

She was crouched inside a short tunnel. It was a good hiding spot. She would have been hard to find, and even harder to catch.

That is, if anyone had bothered to look.

Holly curled her legs, her feet propped up on the blue plastic wall of the tunnel. She frowned, crossing her arms, trying to stop her bottom lip from quivering.

She should have known better. No one *ever* wanted to play with her. But then today, out of the blue, the other kids asked if she wanted to play hide-and-seek. Owen Orlofsky, wiping his nose with his hand. Karen Graham, always blinking super slowly because everyone said what long eyelashes she had. Zoe Zamarripa, the tallest in their class, standing with her hands on her hips like some sort of drill sergeant. They were all smiling and giggling and giving one another knowing looks.

Thinking back, it was so obvious. None of those kids had ever liked her.

But Hector was with them. Hector, her younger brother by a year.

Did he know what they had planned?

Now everyone was gone. They had all left her in the park, alone. It had been a trick. They'd never wanted to play with her. They just wanted to have a laugh at the nerdy girl without any friends.

It hadn't always been like this. She used to have friends. She thought she did, at least. The memories weren't clear, more of a feeling—other kids around her, at recess, at birthday parties. And she and Hector had been insepa-rable. But that was a long time ago now.

Holly heard the wind pick up again, whistling past the tunnel, and wiped her tear-streaked cheeks. She crawled out of the tunnel and saw something odd.

The trees weren't moving with the wind. Neither were

the leaves on the ground. Even the blades of grass stood still.

A hazy mist crept in, blanketing the park in fog.

A figure emerged from the mist. It was a man, his face hidden by a wild tangle of stringy brown hair. His clothes were dusty and patched up and like something a peasant would have worn hundreds of years ago. He was walking slowly, straight toward Holly, looking right at her.

Holly froze in place.

The man approached. He spoke, his voice rough and coarse. "Holly Thorn," he said.

How does he know my name? Holly thought, too shocked and frightened to respond.

"You hid," the man continued. "But you were not found. You thought you were playing a harmless game." He stepped closer, his voice low and ominous. "You were *wrong.*"

She didn't know what that meant. She just knew that something strange was happening—something strange and terrible—and nothing would ever be the same.

2

HOLLY DID WHAT ANY SENSIBLE PERSON WOULD DO IF A STRANGE, hairy man dressed in raggedy old clothes appeared in a park and began talking nonsense.

She ran.

Her house was only just across the street from the park. She sprinted as fast as she could, yelling, "Help!" as she ran. She looked over her shoulder to see if the man was following her, but the street was empty. There were no people, no cars. Even the birds were silent.

She lived in a redbrick house on the corner. Holly sprinted up the driveway and to the rusty metal gate that was part of the breezeway between her house and the garage. She swung the gate open and ran through the yard to the back door.

She went inside, slammed the door, and locked it.

She should have felt safe. But she didn't.

What had that man been talking about? Where had he

come from? *How did he know my name?* She wiped sweat off her forehead and realized her hands were trembling.

"DAAAAAD!" she screamed. Her voice cracked with panic.

Her dad would be home. He hardly ever left the house these days. *Ever since Mom* . . . Holly shook her head. She couldn't start thinking about that right now.

She ran through the house to her dad's office. The door was closed, which meant she wasn't supposed to bother him. She twisted the doorknob and slammed her shoulder against the door anyway, busting into the room.

Her dad was at his desk, where he always was, hunched over his computer. He was tall and thin, and over the last month or two, he had gotten even thinner. His arms, once tanned and freckled by the sun, were now pale. He sat engulfed by stacks of files and papers. They cluttered his desk, piled high against the walls, and even surrounded his chair. It was as if he had literally walled himself in with his work.

He didn't look up when Holly crashed into the room.

"Dad!" Holly said from the doorway, her heart still pounding. "Dad, something happened! There was a man! DAD!"

He didn't respond. His eyes stayed locked on his computer while he typed with a single index finger, hunting and pecking each keystroke.

Holly knew he had been getting lost in his work, but this was ridiculous. Couldn't he tell how upset she was?

5

She strode into the room, not caring that she knocked over a file or two on her way to his desk.

"Dad, *listen*," she pleaded. "Please, come on, this is serious."

She tugged at his arm. It wouldn't budge. It was like tugging at a statue.

"DAD!" Holly screamed, right in his ear. He didn't react. He stayed slouched over his computer, continuing to work as if Holly weren't there. Holly put her hands on his cheeks, like she used to do when she was little. She felt stubble prickling her fingers. He hadn't shaved. "Please, Dad, stop ignoring me, please!"

"He can't hear you," a voice said from behind.

Holly turned. It was the man from the park. He was here. He was in her house.

The man loomed in the doorway. He was more than six feet tall and glowered down at Holly with brown eyes so spotted and stormy they had the color of fossilized amber. His face was tan and weathered, and he had a wild, bushy mustache so large it obscured his mouth. Dirt was everywhere—smudged and streaked on his nose, on his clothes, and under his fingernails.

Holly screamed. She grabbed her dad again. *"That's him!"* she yelled, and pulled at her dad with all her might.

"I told you," the man said, stepping forward, making a little *tsk* sound with his tongue. "He can't hear you. Can't see you. Can't even feel you."

He put a hand in front of her dad's face and waved it up and down, back and forth. Her dad just kept sitting there.

"See?" he said.

"DAD!" Holly screamed again.

The man raised his eyebrows, making his eyes wide. "He doesn't even *remember* you."

Holly searched her dad's face for any sign, any hint that he might be aware of what was happening around him. There was none.

"What's happening?" Holly asked, backing away, trying to get some distance from this man who had invaded her house. "Who are you?"

"My name is Oliver." He knelt on one knee, putting himself at Holly's level. "And you've got two choices. Stay here and be forever invisible. Forever forgotten. Or come with me."

Oliver waited for her to respond. His eyes were sad and intense, and he smelled earthy and funky.

Holly wanted nothing more than to run out of the room and as far away from him as humanly possible. There was so much she didn't understand right now. She didn't understand how this man had gotten inside her house or what he was doing there. She didn't understand why her dad couldn't see her. Why couldn't he feel her yanking his arm? Why couldn't he hear her screams?

But through all that confusion and panic, there was one thing she did know. It was the simplest of lessons, one that

7

had been drilled into her head a thousand times over—never, *ever* go anywhere with a stranger. And this man was nothing if not a stranger.

"No," Holly said. "I'm not going anywhere with you."

"You'd rather stay here?" Oliver asked.

"Yes," she answered. "Yes, I want to stay here."

Oliver stood up. "Oh, no you don't," he said, shaking his head. "You don't want to stay *here*. Here is where everyone you know will walk right by you. Never noticing your tears. Never hearing your cries for help. Here is where you will be stuck, helpless, watching everyone go about their lives as if you never even existed. No, you do not want to stay here. You want to go *back*."

"Back?" Holly asked. "Back where?"

"Back to the way it was *before*," he said. He lowered his voice, seeming sad. "I understand. You want to be with your family. But there's only one way to do that." Oliver leaned down and held his hand out, inviting Holly to take it.

She stared at his outstretched hand, his palm lined with dirt and grime. Nothing that was happening made any sense. Nothing this man had said made any sense. Holly put her hands behind her back. She turned her head, looking away.

She wasn't going anywhere.

3

"HMPH," OLIVER SNORTED. HE SLAPPED HIS HANDS ON HIS KNEES
and stood up straight. "Have it your way," he said, frowning
in a way that managed to convey both disappointment and
contempt. He moved Holly aside with one arm and edged
past her. With his shoulders slumped and his head bowed,
he walked across the room and out the door.

Holly stood still as she listened to his footsteps retreat
down the hall. She heard the front door open and close.

Did he really just leave? Just like that? Could this night-
mare actually be over?

She turned back to her father. "Dad," she said quietly,
trying one last time. Again, she was only met with silence.

Her dad wouldn't be able to help her.

What about Hector? Where was he? Should she go look
for him?

But then she remembered how he had looked at the

park. Surrounded by the other kids, smiling. Practically giddy, really. The reason why was obvious now.

He had been excited. He knew what they had planned. He *had* to have known.

No, Holly told herself. Hector wasn't going to be any help, whether she could find him or not. She'd have to figure this out on her own.

She left her dad's office and peeked into the hallway. The man, Oliver, was nowhere to be seen.

But something wasn't quite right. It was something Holly hadn't noticed when she had sprinted through her house before. The hallway looked *different*. It was impossible, but somehow, the hallway was *longer*.

She had been up and down this hall countless times and knew the layout of the house as well as she knew anything. Mom and Dad's room was at the end, the door shut, as usual. Holly's and Hector's rooms were on the left. A bathroom and her dad's office were on the right.

Except now there was an additional door. A whole new room, one she had never seen before. The door was closed.

She walked toward this strange new door. She was about to go in when she heard the thump of boxes being moved in her parents' room. Mom was up.

Maybe she can help, Holly thought. *Maybe she'll snap out of it.* She knew that wasn't likely. Mom hadn't been herself lately. But the urge to see her, to run to her, was overwhelming.

Holly charged into her parents' room, slamming the door open with a loud thud.

The room was dark. The shades were drawn over the window, light from outside peeking in around the edges. The room looked like it had been ransacked. But that was typical these days. Dresser drawers lay open, clothes strewn about haphazardly.

Her mom was on her hands and knees, rummaging around inside the closet. Holly could hear her shifting boxes and sliding wire hangers out of the way.

Mom was in sweatpants and a T-shirt. In the last month or so, she had rarely worn anything else. Her skin—the same olive brown complexion shared by Holly and Hector—looked dry and sallow. Her black hair was in a loose, unraveling braid. Holly instinctively touched her own neat braid of dark hair—they had been wearing their hair the same way for years now.

"Mom?" Holly said.

Even if she could hear her, Holly knew her mom wasn't likely to respond. She had been lost in her own world for weeks. When she wasn't sleeping, she was looking, searching. Practically tearing the house inside out, room by room.

"Something's missing," she would say. *"I know it. Something's missing."* It was about all she said these days.

But Mom never found anything. She just kept looking. Dad had taken her to see doctors. When that didn't work, relatives and neighbors were full of advice. *Have you tried music? Meditation? Does she take vitamins?*

Their next-door neighbor, Mrs. Murphy, said the same thing had happened to her cousin, years ago. She even had a name for it. She called it "the Missing."

That's what she's got, Mrs. Murphy had said, kneading her cat's fur with her knuckles. *It's the town curse. Been happening to folks here in Covenant since before my nana's time.*

Dad had thanked Mrs. Murphy but told Holly she was just superstitious as they walked away.

"Mom," Holly said again. She went to her and touched her shoulder. Just like with Dad, there was no response. "Please, Mom." Holly clutched her mom's sweatshirt in a fist. "I need you. I need you back *now.*"

Nothing.

Holly heard a door creaking open in the hallway. Her dad emerged from his office. He looked tired. He paused in front of the family portrait hanging in the hallway, yawned, and scratched his head, then walked away. She followed him. He went down the hall, through the living room, and into the kitchen.

Her dad began pulling ingredients out of the pantry for dinner. It looked like spaghetti. Again.

But then he stopped. He put a hand on top of his head and rubbed, his expression knotting up in confusion. He got on his knees and reached inside a cabinet, rummaging, metal pots and pans clanking against one another. Only the back half of his body was visible as he dug deeper and deeper inside, as though he was looking for something he couldn't find.

Just like Mom.

"You can't help me." Holly frowned. "Can you, Dad?"

There was no answer.

The strange man, Oliver, had been right. They couldn't see her. They couldn't hear her.

Holly took one last look down the hallway, toward her mom.

She felt tears welling up and rubbed her eyes. No. She wasn't going to cry.

Instead, she turned around and walked out of the kitchen. There was only one person who could help her now.

4

HOLLY OPENED THE FRONT DOOR. SHE HESITATED, STANDING AT the threshold between her house and the front yard. Inside, she could still hear the faint sounds of her dad searching in the kitchen cabinets. Outside, waiting for her, was Oliver.

He was at the curb in front of her house. Next to him, in the street, were two huge, shaggy, horned farm animals. Probably oxen, Holly guessed. They were hitched to a simple wagon that consisted of two giant spoked wheels and a wooden bed to sit on. Or haul things in, she supposed.

Like terrified children.

Oliver leaned against the cart with his arms crossed. He saw Holly, gave her a sour frown, and nodded.

"Changed your mind," he said. It wasn't a question.

"Yes." Holly nodded back.

Holly closed the door to her house and went down the walkway to Oliver and his oxen. The reason for the odor that hung about Oliver was suddenly obvious. The oxen smelled terrible. Oliver began gently patting the beasts, who didn't seem to acknowledge his presence in any way.

"You ready?" he asked, motioning for her to climb aboard. Up close, the cart looked like it was practically falling apart.

Holly bit her lip. It was time to pull herself together. It didn't matter how rough and strange Oliver looked, or that he rode around on an oxcart, of all things. She had to set things right, and he was the only one who knew how to do that. No more panicking. She had to have a clear mind. She had to *think*.

"One question," Holly said. "You said there was a way to change everything back. How? What do I have to do?"

Oliver peered down at her, his dark brown eyes looking as wild as his unkempt hair. "You have to play," he said.

"Play?" Holly asked. "Play what?"

"The game," Oliver answered.

"That's not terribly specific," Holly said before she could stop herself. She sometimes had a terrible habit of just blurting out exactly what she was thinking. It was probably one of the reasons she had such trouble making friends.

Oliver narrowed his eyes at her. "*None* of the other children have spoken to me like that," he growled.

Holly's eyes lit up. *Other children. He's done this before.* "You probably scared them," Holly said, again not thinking. "Er, what I meant to say is . . . where are we going?"

"You are already there," Oliver told her.

Holly looked around. She didn't see anything out of the ordinary. It was just her neighborhood—single-story ranch homes with tidy, well-manicured lawns, the sidewalks lined with trees.

"You now belong to a place that is *hidden*," Oliver said. "Someplace forgotten, for the forgotten. Someplace lost, for the lost. The *Hiddenseek*."

"The Hiddenseek," Holly repeated. "But I can get back. To the normal world. Right? You told me that I could."

Oliver hesitated. It didn't seem like he wanted to answer. Finally, though, he spoke. "Yes. It is possible."

"OK. How do I do that?"

"There is only one way to answer all the questions you have," Oliver said. He motioned toward his oxcart. "There is only one path forward."

Holly looked back at her house. The red brick, the big windows framed by black shutters, the lawn with its patches of clover. This was home. *This* was where she was safe.

But inside were parents who couldn't see or hear her. And what about Hector? She guessed he would forget about her too. Would she ever see him again? Where was he? Was he still with those *other* kids?

A feeling that had been growing in her gut finally took shape. It was *Hector's* fault she was in this mess, stuck in whatever the Hiddenseek was. She was put here— *betrayed*—by her own brother.

And now she was invisible. Now she was forgotten.

Well, she thought, *not for long.*

Oliver had said there was a way back. All she had to do was play some game. She could do that.

"OK," she said, looking Oliver square in the eyes. "Let's go."

He held out a hand to help her up, but Holly ignored it and leapt onto the oxcart by herself. The loose wooden planks of the rickety cart trembled under her weight.

Oliver grunted and let out a dirty, nasal snort—the similarities between him and his oxen weren't limited to their smell. He didn't get in the cart, though, as Holly expected. Instead, he started walking back to her house.

"Hey!" she called to him. "Where are you going?"

"I require one last thing," he said as he opened her front door. "I need your brother."

5

HECTOR HID.

He was at home, in a room that shouldn't exist.

The fact that there was an extra room in the house, one that had never been there before, should have alarmed Hector. It was impossible, wasn't it? But this new room was not the most impossible thing that had happened today. Not by a long shot.

It had been a very strange day.

Hector thought back to when all the weirdness had begun and immediately felt a rush of shame. He had been so excited. He was finally going to show Holly. He was finally going to *outsmart* her. The prank had been his idea, and everyone else had been more than happy to play along.

All they had to do was ask her to play hide-and-seek.

Afterward, his friends ran off to do something else. But Hector snuck back to the park. He wanted to see Holly. He wanted to see the look on her face when she realized she'd been tricked.

He hid behind one of the benches. Peering between the wooden slats, he watched Holly emerge from her hiding place.

When he saw her, though, Hector's smile disintegrated. The elation he had been feeling immediately curdled into guilt and regret.

Holly's face was red. Her cheeks were wet with tears. She'd been crying.

Oh, man, he thought. *I think I messed up.*

He watched her standing there, looking sad and hurt and alone. He considered stepping out from behind the bench and going to her. But what would he say? That it was just a joke? Could he lie and say it was somebody else's idea? *She'd see right through that.*

He didn't want to face her. Not yet.

Hiding seemed like a good idea. He would continue to hide.

That was when the man showed up.

Hector immediately knew something was off about him. With his old, dirty clothes and tangled mess of hair, he looked like he'd just rolled out of the gutter. When Holly ran away and the man started walking after her, Hector knew he had to follow.

He was careful to stay a good distance behind, so he

wouldn't be seen. He crept along, watching as the man tromped across their lawn and around to the front of their house.

What was he going to do, ring the doorbell? Kick the front door down?

Hector had to know what this man was up to. He crawled into the bushes that ran along the side of the house. He would use them as cover, peek around the corner, and get a look at their front porch.

He poked his head out and found himself face-to-face with the strange man.

"Hector Thorn," the man said.

"Yagh!" Hector responded, completely startled.

"You thought you were playing a harmless game. You were *wrong*."

"I'm sorry!" Hector yelped. He didn't really know why he was apologizing.

What was he supposed to do now? *C'mon, think,* he admonished himself. *What would Holly do?*

She'd ask questions.

"What are you doing here?" Hector demanded. "Who are you?"

"The name's Oliver," the man answered. "And you've got two choices. Stay here and be forever invisible. Forever forgotten. Or come with me."

"Sure," Hector said.

"Oh." Oliver widened his eyes. "But you don't want to

stay *here*. Here is . . ." He stopped, scratching his head vigorously, like he had fleas. "Wait. Did you say yes?"

"Yeah." Hector smiled. "Sounds good."

Hector had no intention of going anywhere with this guy. But he also knew arguing with adults was stupid. They never changed their minds about anything. Better to agree with them, wait until they got distracted—which never took long—and then go do whatever you were going to do in the first place.

Oliver bent over and grabbed Hector under his arms.

The smell was unbearable. *This dude STINKS,* Hector thought. *Like the stink-of-a-thousand-butts stink.* He had never wanted to hold his nose more in his entire life.

Oliver carried Hector to the curb in front of their house. There were two big ugly animals there, both of them yoked to an old wooden cart.

Oliver put Hector down on the cart. "Wait here," he said. "I will be back with your sister." Then he went up the walkway to the house and stepped inside.

Hector couldn't believe his luck.

He hopped out of the cart. Now he could just run off and get as far away from that smelly weirdo as possible.

But Holly's still in there.

Oliver said he was going to get his sister. Hector couldn't just leave her. Especially after what he'd done.

Hector tiptoed inside, first checking out the kitchen. It was a mess, as usual these days. Stacks of dirty dishes were in the sink. Chip bags and cereal boxes cluttered the counters. The fridge, as always, was covered in little magnets holding up tests and essays, all with perfect scores. All of them Holly's. A shrine to her brilliance. Nothing of Hector's up there, also as usual.

There was no sign of his sister or Oliver.

I should call 911, Hector thought.

He checked the counter over the junk drawer, where Mom and Dad kept everything from pens and pencils to tape and batteries to rubber bands and other stuff that didn't belong anywhere else. There used to be a phone there, an old landline. But Dad had gotten rid of it.

No, Hector suddenly remembered. *He didn't get rid of the phone. He moved it. To his office.*

Hector quietly made his way to the hall, but when he got near the office, he stopped. The door was open. It was never open. Then he heard voices.

"Here is where you will be stuck, helpless, watching everyone go about their lives as if you never even existed." It was Oliver's voice, coming from the office. "No, you do not want to stay here. You want to go *back.*"

Was Oliver talking to Dad? Why wasn't Dad talking back?

Then Hector noticed the picture.

It was their family picture, the only one on the wall. They had taken it a few years ago, one of those cheesy studio portraits.

Hector remembered the whole ordeal perfectly. How Mom had made Holly wear a dress, which she hated. How he kept sliding off his stool, trying to escape. How Mom and Dad tried to bribe them into compliance, all while maintaining perfect, forced smiles.

Every shot the photographer took was a disaster. Naturally it became everyone's favorite Thorn family photo, something that never failed to make them laugh.

Except now the picture was different.

There were two other kids in it.

Everything else was as it should be. There was Hector, halfway off the stool, right next to Holly looking all slouchy and miserable. Dad was there, a stressed-out smile plastered on his face. And there was Mom. But next to her were two boys. They were older kids, both of them almost as tall as Mom. The camera had caught them fighting, trying to elbow each other.

"Back? Back where?"

Hector jumped. *That's Holly,* he realized. He snuck to the open doorway, poking his head just around the edge to get a look.

Big, hairy Oliver was looming over Holly. He was holding his hand out to her. Holly shied away like his hand was diseased and contagious.

Dad was at his desk, clacking away at his keyboard as if nothing at all were amiss.

"Hmph. Have it your way," Oliver said.

Then he sighed and stood up straight. He took a step back.

Hector froze as he realized what was happening. *He's coming!* his mind screamed, trying to jolt his petrified body into action. *Hide!* Hector's legs finally got the message, and he rushed down the hall, scrambling to his room. He swung the door open and at the last second remembered to shut it gently, quietly behind him. Then he gasped.

This room had a bunk bed. The walls were lined with bookshelves, all of which were overflowing with books. There were zero toys.

This isn't my room, he realized. It wasn't any room he had ever seen in his life. *What in the world is this?*

The sound of footsteps in the hallway spurred him into action. He had to hide, and there wasn't time to get creative. He dropped to his stomach and squirmed under the bed. It was a tight squeeze, but there was just enough room for him.

He waited. He strained to hear if anything was happening in the house. He heard some bumps, maybe a cabinet opening. He thought he heard voices. He couldn't be sure.

Long minutes went by. He wanted to get out, to run, but he didn't dare move.

At last, he heard footsteps again in the hallway. They got louder and louder—someone was coming, getting close.

From under the bed, Hector could see the door open and a pair of filthy, tattered boots stomp into the room. There was no question who they belonged to.

"Come out, Hector Thorn," Oliver said. "Your sister is waiting."

6

HOLLY SAT IN THE OXCART. SHE WATCHED THE FRONT DOOR, waiting for Oliver to come back out but dreading his return.

Was Hector really inside this whole time? she wondered.

Part of her wanted to see him. Part of her hoped he was somewhere else, somewhere safe. And then there was another part of her that was still angry.

They're all probably still laughing at you. If they remember you at all.

The front door opened. Out walked Oliver. Next to him, looking scared and confused, was Hector. He saw her and ran to the oxcart.

"Holly!" he said, stopping just short, putting his hands on the edge.

"Hector," she sighed.

The anger she'd been feeling went away. What she

felt now more than anything was relief. He knew who she was. He could see her. She hadn't been totally forgotten by everyone she knew.

"Hey, dummy," she said, using her pet name for him.

"Holly, what's happening?" Hector asked. "I saw Dad. Why didn't he say anything?"

"I don't know," she said. "It was the same with me."

"That man said we have to go with him?" He craned his neck around, checking both ways down the street, as if looking for help.

Before she could answer, Oliver came up behind Hector, lifted him by the armpits, and set him down next to Holly. Then he pulled himself onto the cart, stepping up in one quick motion. He nudged Hector and Holly aside with his hip.

"Time to go," Oliver said.

Hector's face crumpled. He looked ready to cry.

"We're going to be OK," she told him.

He wouldn't look at her. Tears began to slip from his eyes. He was melting down. She had to help him keep it together, or they'd never make it out of this. She put her hands on his shoulders, bringing her face close to his.

"Come on," she whispered to him. "We can do this."

He nodded. "Yeah." He wiped his nose with his sleeve. "OK."

Oliver leaned over and gave one of the oxen a pat on the

back. The animal grunted, and the pair started pulling the wobbly, creaking wagon slowly forward.

"Where are we going?" Holly asked. "I thought you said that we were already there."

"Yes," Oliver said curtly.

She could see that he was getting annoyed, but she kept talking anyway. "So where are you taking us?"

"Crossroads," Oliver said, and pointed to the four-way stop at the corner.

Holly looked. Everything still seemed ordinary. There was just the road, the green street signs with familiar names, and a red stop sign.

The oxcart continued to scrape slowly along, over a speed bump. *It would have been easier to walk,* Holly thought.

"So . . . no cars where you're from? Or, like . . . bicycles?" she asked. She really couldn't help herself.

"Try not to speak," Oliver said. He didn't look at them, instead keeping his eyes on the road ahead. "You should be preparing."

Holly didn't like the sound of that. "Preparing? How? For what?"

Now Oliver did turn to them. He looked stern. "Some children panic when they see . . . certain things. They can't handle it." He gave Holly and Hector a knowing look and tapped his head with his finger. "That's why I said prepare."

Holly felt her stomach drop. Maybe they should have stayed home after all. She turned around toward their house. They hadn't gone that far. She could still jump out and run back.

"Best to hold on," Oliver said.

They reached the crossroads, and the wind shifted.

It was sharp and fierce, whipping across Holly's face. She was surprised to find the air pummeling her cheeks was crisp and cool. Only seconds ago, the weather had been warm. Hector's wavy hair flapped in the wind.

Next came the fog. It drifted down and settled over the houses and trees, its misty tendrils shrouding the whole neighborhood in gray. The road ahead was now impossible to see, obscured in a cloud.

The hair on Holly's arms stood up, and not just from the cold.

"What's happening?" Hector asked, his voice barely more than a whisper.

The oxcart jolted, like they had hit a pothole.

Oliver wasn't answering. He kept his eyes forward, a grim resolve on his face. She noticed he was gripping the edge of the wagon. His knuckles were white.

Another bump, and the oxcart began to roll and bounce faster. Holly felt herself leaning forward. They were going downhill. But that didn't make sense. There were no hills in her neighborhood.

They went faster still. The two oxen shambled forward,

their stout hooves struggling to keep pace with their own momentum. One of them grunted.

Scenery raced by. Through the mist, Holly saw fewer and fewer houses, and more and more trees. Different trees—not the familiar oaks and maples she knew so well, but towering trees with outstretched limbs that brushed the sky. The ground was no longer asphalt but dirt.

The road ahead was still a mass of fog. And they were rushing right into it. Her entire body rumbled and shook along with the oxcart as they careened downward into the unknown wilderness.

Hector squeezed her hand so hard that it hurt, but she didn't let go, holding on to him just as fiercely. With her other hand she gripped her seat tighter, her stomach lurching as they bowled downhill like rocks in a landslide.

Then they stopped.

7

HOLLY JERKED FORWARD AT THEIR ABRUPT STOP, AND FOR A split second she thought she was going to go flying out of the oxcart. But an outstretched arm caught her and Hector both. It was Oliver, who had obviously anticipated what would happen. She got the sense that this was all routine to him, that he had done it many times before.

Oliver leapt off the cart, his scraggly mane of hair bouncing in the air. Then he reached and picked Hector up and set him on the ground. Holly jumped down by herself.

"We have arrived," he said.

Holly took in their surroundings. They were in a forest of impossibly tall trees. So many trees—all fir or spruce or pine, with their long, naked trunks and pointy, prickly leaves. The fog had cleared, but the forest was so thick that all was cast in shadow, even though it was still daylight. Beneath her shoes the ground was damp and mossy. Some rustling in the brush revealed a squirrel. It scurried away.

"Where are we?" Holly asked. How could a forest suddenly appear out of nowhere? Where was her neighborhood? How were they going to get back home?

Oliver knelt to meet her and Hector at eye level. "I am going to tell you what I have told every child I bring to the Hiddenseek." His voice had turned somber. His eyes were glazed, like he was daydreaming. "There is a way out," he said. "But you won't make it." He blinked, emerging from his trance, and locked eyes with Holly. "No one ever has."

Holly began to panic. "That's not what you said. You said we could get back. If we play."

Oliver stood up and brushed off his knee. He was all business again. "It starts with counting," he said, putting a hand on his oxcart. It looked like he was getting ready to climb back on.

Is he leaving us here?

"Listen for the count," he continued. "You will not have much time to hide." He climbed aboard.

"Wait!" Holly called after him. "Where do we go? What are we supposed to do?"

From somewhere deep inside the forest, a bell rang. A single clang. Its tone was muted and flat, like it was covered in a shroud. A moment later it rang again. This time twice in a row.

"She is coming," Oliver said as the oxen began to move. He had a strange look on his face. It seemed like pity. "*It* is coming." He nodded at them. "Whether you are ready or not."

Then he and his oxen rolled away, disappearing into the forest.

The bell kept ringing. Three times. Then four. Then five.

It starts with counting, Holly thought. All at once, the pieces fit together. The counting. His last words to her. *Whether you are ready or not.*

It was so obvious.

"Hector," she said.

"Huh?"

"Of all the stupid tricks to play on me," she said, "why did it have to be hide-and-seek?"

The count was in the double digits now, the continuous ringing sounding like an alarm.

Holly spun around, trying to decide what to do. They were surrounded by trees, long and foreboding. There was nothing but shadow and the unknown in every direction. She didn't know which way to turn.

The ringing stopped.

The sudden quiet was unnerving. Now there was just the wind and the rustling of foliage and the faint chittering of hidden wildlife.

Then, from somewhere behind them, a slow, mournful wail broke through the woods. It was barely more than a whimper at first, but it quickly grew louder, stronger. The cry was ghostly and eerie, and worst of all, it was *close*.

"What was that?" Hector asked.

"Run," Holly said.

"What?"

Holly grabbed Hector's hand. "RUN!"

She sprinted away, charging into the gloom of the forest, dragging Hector with her. She sidestepped and dodged trees as she ran, not daring to break her stride or slow down.

All she saw in front of her were more trees, nothing that could conceal them from whatever had made that awful sound. She kept running, all the while looking for somewhere to hide, for anyplace that could keep them safe.

AROOOOOO!!!!!

Another cry from behind, this one not a forlorn moaning but instead a soul-rattling howl. Like something was calling out to her but also shrieking in pain.

Holly looked behind her. In the distance, she saw two eyes, red and glowing. They were the eyes of an animal on the hunt, and they were staring right at her. Those eyes saw her, she could tell. They shone with the recognition of exactly who and what Holly was.

She was their prey.

"Hector," she said. "Climb that tree."

"What?"

It was all she could think of. Whatever that red-eyed thing was, she hoped it couldn't climb.

She pulled Hector over to a bent and ancient birch tree. This would be easier to climb than the tall pine trees that dominated the forest. The lowest branch was still fairly high off the ground, though.

"Here," she said, "I'll give you a boost." She bent over and joined her hands together. Hector hesitated, so she snapped at him. "*Now.*"

He put his foot in her hands. As she boosted him up, he stretched for the branch and grabbed it, pulling himself onto the tree.

"C'mon." He reached a hand down, ready to help pull her up.

Holly stood on her tiptoes and stretched her arms. Their hands didn't touch. She tried jumping, but she couldn't get high enough. He was just barely out of reach.

"Try climbing the trunk," Hector said.

She started toward the base of the tree, but a deep, guttural growl stopped her in her tracks.

It was too late.

She turned to see the animal step slowly out of the shadows of the forest. It was a wolf. Its fur was completely black. There wasn't a single spot of gray or white, as if the beast had been coated in midnight. Its red eyes were like two burning embers.

"Run, Holly!" Hector screamed at her. "RUN!"

Holly ran for her life.

8

HOLLY TORE THROUGH THE WOODS AS FAST AS SHE COULD. No longer trying to dodge trees, she banged her elbows and shoulders against their trunks, collecting cuts and bruises that she didn't even slow down to acknowledge.

She could hear the wolf moving fast behind her, so Holly had to run faster, her chest heaving and tears coming to her eyes.

The ground was getting uneven, and Holly stumbled. Tall grass and spindly branches slapped at her legs and waist, slowing her down. There was too much shrubbery; there were too many trees. She couldn't see ahead.

Suddenly, there was nothing under her feet. She was falling, skidding on her elbows, tumbling down into the dirt. She landed hard on her back.

"Ow," she said.

She listened. There was no sound of pursuit, no moaning or howling.

I have to make my way back to Hector, she thought, picking herself off the ground. That's when she noticed what was right in front of her. It was not what she expected.

The forest had thinned out. There was a thin line of trees, and just beyond that, the woods gave way to a sprawling field. The clearing was wide—as big as a soccer field, at least. Strange objects were scattered all over the clearing, but Holly couldn't quite make out what they were from a distance.

Then she noticed something else. At the edge of the field, squatting with their backs against a tree, were two other kids.

They were far enough away that they hadn't noticed Holly emerge from the forest. She quietly inched her way toward them. One was a boy with frayed holes in his jeans and T-shirt. His skin was a sandy brown, a touch lighter than Holly's, and his dark brown hair was matted with sweat and grime. The other was a girl, fair-skinned, also in jeans, with a purple shirt. Her hair was blond at the roots but sprouted out in a rainbow of bright pink and blue.

As she got near, she could hear them whispering back and forth, their voices straining to stay quiet. They were arguing.

"He's *right there*," the boy said. He glanced around the tree and out into the field. "This is our chance."

"You heard the bell," the girl responded. Her voice was tight with fear. "Don't be stupid!"

Holly hesitated, instinctively reluctant to insert herself where she might not be wanted. But the red-eyed wolf might still be chasing her, and these kids might know something. She darted forward, grass and dead leaves crunching under her shoes.

They turned at the sound of Holly approaching. Holly skidded to a stop and crouched down. They gawked at her.

"Holly?" the boy said, his voice full of disbelief.

"Max? You *know* her?" the girl asked.

"Huh?" Holly replied. *How does he know my name?* She studied his face, his dark brown eyes, the mole on his right cheek, searching for any sign of familiarity. She had never seen this boy before in her life. "Um, yes, I'm Holly." She didn't know what else to say.

"You don't . . ." the boy began, then shook his head. "Never mind. Of course you don't. What are you doing here?"

"Keep your voices down," the girl hissed. "We have to go. *Now.*"

"Wait." Max pointed. "Look."

They looked.

Holly gasped. Now that she was closer, she could finally make out what those strange things in the field actually were.

They were statues, scattered across the clearing like tombstones in a graveyard.

They didn't look like normal statues, though. Each

one showed a person in some sort of distress. Some were cowering on the ground, their heads between their knees. Some were looking to the sky, their arms covering their faces, as if trying to shield their eyes. One looked like a girl who was running, her legs in midstride, but the statue had toppled over onto the ground.

All of the statues were short.

Not just short, Holly realized. *They're kids. They're all kids.*

And then she saw movement. Huddled next to one of the statues was a boy. He looked younger than Holly, maybe Hector's age. His skin was so pale it practically glowed. But the most striking thing about him was his hair. It was gray.

The boy saw them. He waved. Holly couldn't be sure, but it looked like he was smiling. Then he ducked behind the statue, disappearing from view.

"Unbelievable," Max said through gritted teeth. Then he turned to Holly. His expression was pained, almost desperate. "I'll be right back. Stay here. This is our best shot at getting home."

"Don't." The girl reached for him, but Max didn't seem to notice. He sprang up and bolted into the open field.

"Max!" the girl called after him, but it was no use. He sprinted away, taking big, clumsy strides toward the statue where the gray-haired boy was hiding.

He made it to the statue and tumbled down. He got on

his hands and knees, crawling around, searching. He made a full circle around the statue. No one was there.

Then the statue's eyes glowed red, sparking like a flare.

AROOOOOOO!

From behind them came a howl.

The girl in the purple shirt grabbed Holly's arm. She squeezed so hard it hurt.

"Get low," the girl whispered. "Hide."

Holly heard something burst out of the greenery above the ridge. She turned to see the wolf in midair, leaping down in a streak of fur and fangs. It landed in stride and charged in their direction.

Holly sat with her back against the tree, frozen in place. The girl next to her lay flat, her belly on ground.

The wolf raced toward them. Its white fangs flashed as it got closer and closer.

There was nowhere Holly could run to, no time to move or hide. She closed her eyes and thought of her mom, her dad. She thought of Hector, hoping he was safe.

But the beast dashed right past her.

Holly trembled, a spike of fear and relief coursing through her at once. Her heart was pounding. The girl next to her, though, looked anything but relieved. She was staring out into the field, her expression grim and helpless.

"Max," the girl whispered, her voice breaking. The way she said his name sounded sad and final. Like she was saying good-bye.

Holly peeked around the tree. Max was on his hands and knees by the statue, huddling beneath it, clinging to its shadows. And there was the wolf, growling in front of him, taking slow steps closer and closer.

It had him cornered.

Max shook his head back and forth, pleading, "No, no, no."

Then the wolf did something strange.

It rose up on its hind legs. It stretched, its entire body getting longer. Its dark fur rippled across its body, coming loose and billowing out like a cape caught in the wind. The fur became a dress, long and whispery and still utterly black. From the dress's sleeves, naked arms appeared, as pale as moonlight. Where there had once been paws, there were now bare feet. Finally, at the top, the wolf's head disappeared in a silky weave of long black hair. The hair framed a fair face, which, even from a distance, Holly could see was cold and stern.

The wolf had transformed into a woman.

Holly had witnessed it with her own eyes, but she still couldn't believe it.

What is happening? What is this place?

The woman approached Max. He shrank away from her, trying helplessly to make himself small. She reached an arm out, extending two thin fingers. Then she touched him on the head, gently, like she was anointing him.

The woman removed her hand, revealing a spot of gray

on Max's head. The spot began to grow, spreading down his face and past his neck. Every part of him touched by gray became solid and still.

Like a statue.

Soon Max's entire body was gray and motionless. He sat frozen, an expression of terror etched on his face.

The woman's touch had turned him to stone.

Holly quickly ducked back behind the tree. "What happened?" she gasped, her voice trembling. "What is that thing?"

The girl answered, her expression bleak, "You're playing hide-and-seek. And that's *It.*"

9

A GUST OF WIND BLEW ACROSS THE FIELD. THE WOMAN'S DARK hair danced in the breeze, her black dress swelling with air, like a sail in a storm.

Every instinct in Holly's body was telling her to run. But the girl next to her hadn't moved, her eyes still trained on the woman. As if reading Holly's thoughts, the girl held up a hand, telling Holly to wait.

Holly stayed put, peering around the tree to watch, with mounting dread, what the woman in black would do next.

The woman collapsed.

She dropped to her knees. Her body shook, as if struck by a sudden chill. She clutched the ground, digging her fingernails into the dirt. She curled up in pain, holding her stomach like something had grabbed her by the insides and started to twist.

"Now!" The girl pulled Holly up. "Run!" She sprinted back into the forest.

Holly followed the girl, who ran quickly but not wildly through the brush. The girl ran with purpose, occasionally slowing down to change direction. Holly struggled to keep up.

"Wait," Holly panted. "Stop. We have to stop."

The girl came to an abrupt halt.

"What?" she asked. "*It* will be right behind us."

"My brother," Holly tried to explain between gulps of breath. She had never sprinted so much in her life. "He's out here somewhere."

"I'm sorry." The girl shook her head, not without sympathy. "But there's no way we can look for him now. *It* is right behind us, and it'll be dark soon. We have to—"

And then she stopped talking. She put a finger to her lips.

A howl echoed through the woods. It seemed to come from everywhere at once. It didn't sound searching or mournful, like before. This howl was more of a challenge: *I'm coming. I'm coming.*

The girl turned to Holly. "Outta time." She looked all around and then went over to an old tree with low branches gnarled and bent like knuckles. "Up here, quick."

Holly felt a brief surge of hope for Hector. If this girl hid in trees, then maybe that was the best strategy. Maybe he was still OK.

They leapt and began to climb. The girl, with her long limbs, scaled the tree fast, but Holly struggled to get past the lowest-hanging branches. The girl reached down and offered Holly a hand, pulling her up.

They settled on two neighboring branches, close to the trunk. There was some leaf coverage up here, but not much. Anyone who walked by could see them if they thought to look up.

Holly opened her mouth to say so, but the girl stopped her, holding her finger to her lips and shaking her head.

Holly swallowed her words. All she could do was wait.

In the stillness, Holly listened. The forest was alive all around her—insects humming and buzzing, frogs croaking, leaves bristling as their branches bowed to gusts of wind. A trio of squirrels bolted out of some nearby shrubbery and skirted past. Holly swayed on her branch. Each noise wound her nerves tighter and tighter. *Is that her? Is that the wolf?* she wondered. Every slight disturbance caused a brief sting of panic.

Holly heard a soft crunch—something stepping on leaves. Then another. And another.

She heard a rumbling. A growl. It was soft and slow but getting ever so slightly louder, closer.

The wolf was right below them. It had its nose to the ground, sniffing. It paced around the trunk of the tree and then looked up, its red eyes shining.

It had them.

The wolf sat on its haunches and lifted its nose to the sky.

Holly turned to the girl, who just shook her head.

There was nothing they could do.

Then the wolf stood. Its back straightened. Its front legs became arms. Its black fur melted, flowing like ink, forming a dress. She was the woman again.

The woman circled the tree, gently running her fingers across the trunk like she was caressing it, calming it. She stopped and lifted her head. Her face was unnaturally smooth, like all lines and expression had been polished away. She put one hand on a branch, getting ready to climb.

Just then, another sound echoed through the forest. It was light, happy.

It was laughter. Someone was laughing.

Holly saw the girl next to her exhale, the tension deflating from her shoulders. The girl closed her eyes as if in thankful prayer.

Below, the woman in black dropped her hand, her head snapping toward the sound of the laughter. She turned her back on the tree and took a step away.

The woman spread her arms and put a foot forward, almost like she was preparing for a dive. Black feathers sprouted from her arms, becoming wings. Her dress flapped and stretched, forming a tail. Feathers grew across her face, covering her chalky skin, and from their center emerged a black beak, thick and pointy with a slight hook at the end. Through it all she shrank, smaller and smaller, until there was nothing human left.

She had transformed into a raven.

The bird beat its wings. It launched itself, fluttering, rising, its beak pointed up. It climbed higher, past the trees, through the canopy of the forest. Holly heard it squawk, its cry becoming faint and distant as it disappeared into the gray and darkening sky.

"Climb down," the girl said, breaking the silence. "It's safe now."

The girl reached the ground first and stood with her hands on her hips, surveying their surroundings. Holly landed with a thump, almost falling over on her bottom.

"You all right?" The girl raised an eyebrow.

Holly noticed the girl's purple shirt was stained and torn, a yellow number *30* cracked and faded on the front. Her lollipop-colored hair was a wild tangle on her head.

"No," Holly finally answered. "No, I'm not all right."

Holly fell to her knees. She had been running for who knows how long on nothing but fear and panic and adrenaline, and it was all catching up to her.

"Hey! Whoa!" The girl knelt. "C'mon, we can't stop here."

Holly grabbed the girl by her grimy purple shirt. "Where is *here*? Where are we? What's happening?" She clutched her fist tighter, shaking. "Just tell me what's happening."

"Ohhh-kaaay," the girl said, gently but firmly removing Holly's hand from her shirt. "First day. I get it. Let's start over. I'm Petunia. What's your name again?" The girl, Petunia, continued to hold on to Holly's hand.

"Holly," she answered. "I'm Holly."

"OK, great, pleasure's all mine," Petunia said. "But, Holly, you need to get yourself together. Stand up and follow me."

"Follow you where?" Holly asked.

"Someplace safe," Petunia said. She let go of Holly's hand and stood up.

Someplace safe sounded good. But it wasn't what Holly wanted. She wanted to see her dad again, huddled behind the papers on his desk. She wanted her mom. She wanted to find Hector.

"No," Holly said. "I want to go home."

Petunia crouched in front of her. "They don't remember you. You know that. If you're here, you know that." She grabbed Holly's hands and pulled her to her feet.

Holly still felt dizzy, delirious. "But where are we?" she asked again.

"The Hiddenseek," Petunia said, holding her hand out to show Holly the forest. It was getting darker, the day slowly surrendering to the night. "This is home now."

10

"YOU," OLIVER SAID, SCOWLING DOWN AT HECTOR. HE SOUNDED surprised and irritated at the same time. "Unbelievable."

Hector took it as a compliment.

Earlier, he had watched with horror from his hiding spot in the tree as the wolf charged past, chasing Holly into the woods. In seconds, they had both disappeared into the trees, out of sight. Hector could only listen to the frantic crunching of foliage and snapping of twigs as the wolf and his sister tore through the forest, but those noises quickly faded as they got farther and farther away.

What he hadn't heard, thankfully, was any evidence that the wolf had caught up to Holly. *She's safe,* he told himself. *She has to be.*

The only question, then, was what he should do next.

He knew what Holly would want. *Stay right there so I know where to find you.* He could practically hear her saying it.

Hector surveyed his surroundings. He'd never seen so many trees. They swayed and bristled in the wind. The sky was graying, fading into evening. Hector was suddenly aware that he was very much alone.

He climbed down from the tree and took a few tentative steps into the forest. This was the direction Holly had gone. Maybe he could catch up to her. Maybe it wasn't too late.

Then he heard something creaking. He had heard it before.

Why do I know that noise? he wondered.

He followed the sound, coming upon a rutted dirt road that cut a path through the woods.

Two ungainly farm animals clomped into view. They dragged an old, rickety oxcart behind them, carrying the familiar, grumpy-faced Oliver.

The cart stopped, and Oliver climbed down. He looked annoyed, which surprised Hector a little. He could usually get people to smile.

"I thought I told you to hide," Oliver growled.

"I have to find Holly," Hector said. "Do you know which way she went? Can you help me?"

"I have done all I can for you."

"Please," Hector begged. "I have to find her."

"I *told* you—"

"If you could just help me look. I think she went off that way. We could take your cart."

"I am *warning* you—"

"She's probably up a tree. That's where—"

"SHE'S GONE!" Oliver finally erupted, grabbing Hector by the shoulders. "GONE!" His eyes bulged in boiling anger. "Again and again and again! It never stops! How many of you fools must I take?" Droplets of spit flew from his mouth and clung to his mustache.

Hector shrank away. Oliver seemed to be looking right through him, like he was looking at someone else.

"Olly . . ." a voice sang in the distance. *"Olly-Olly-Olly oxen-free . . ."*

Then there was laughter, a high-pitched, singsong laugh. *A child's voice,* Hector realized. There was another kid in the forest.

Oliver twisted around, craning his neck left and right, trying to determine which way the voice was coming from. "You know better than that!" he shouted into the forest.

There was no reply.

Oliver climbed onto the cart and smacked the back of one of his oxen. "Go on!" he ordered. "Move!"

The beasts heaved forward, pulling Oliver and the cart away. He didn't look back once as he rolled into the woods, at last disappearing in the brush.

Soon all was quiet again.

"Hello?" Hector called, trying to peer into the dusky woods. "Is anyone there? Holly?"

That's probably too much to hope for, Hector thought.

Holly wouldn't be that easy to find. He was going to have to look.

The forest was a maze of trees. He began to feel disoriented right away. The wind whistled and whipped the leaves. Some birds fluttered from the branches of a nearby tree. And then, from somewhere up ahead, another sound pierced the stillness of the woods.

AROOOOO!

It was a howl, held long and loud.

It was the wolf. And it was close.

Hector went from a brisk walk to a trot. The shadows deepened as the sun dropped farther. The forest seemed to surround him, closing in.

Holly, where are you? Hector needed her now. She would know what to do. She always did.

He heard laughter again. It was almost like someone was laughing at *him*.

"*Come out, come out, wherever you are,*" the laughing voice sang.

With that, Hector ran.

He didn't get far. He'd sprinted only a few desperate strides into the forest's thickening darkness when something caught his leg. He tripped, skidding and tumbling into a heap, the ground scraping his knees and hands.

Hector opened his eyes to see someone standing over him. It was a boy, about his own age. He was bent over, his face hovering right in front of Hector's. The boy's eyes and hair were both a soft, ghostly shade of gray.

"Hello," the boy said. "I'm Edmond." He reached out a hand, smiling at Hector. "Want to play?"

11

HOLLY AND PETUNIA TRAVELED THROUGH THE FOREST. PETUNIA said to move slowly, carefully. She told Holly to not draw too much attention to herself by running and stomping everywhere. Holly felt a rush of embarrassment at the advice. This was hide-and-seek, and she had been tromping through the forest like a deranged elephant, smashing leaves and snapping twigs, making all sorts of noise. She should have known to be quiet.

Petunia, it turned out, was full of advice. With the woman in black no longer chasing them, it was like someone had uncorked a bottle: "Watch your step there. Can't carry you if you turn your ankle. Happened to my cousin Brian once. Ankle swelled up like a grapefruit, not that there are any grapefruits around here. Gotta learn to forage. There's no grocery store round the block, or any blocks either, for that matter. Getting harder to see now with the sun going down, so come on."

Petunia stepped over a piece of deadwood on the ground, pointing at it so that Holly wouldn't trip. "Yeah, I was just like you when I got here. Scared, lost, running stupid." Holly flushed with shame again, but Petunia smiled at her. "Don't worry. Everyone freaks out. 'Cept the twins, of course. They found me, showed me how to hide and get food and water and not make such a racket and everything." She frowned. "I don't know how I'm going to tell Marco about Max."

Holly surmised that Marco must be Max's twin brother. She still wondered about Max's strange reaction to her. How had he known her name?

"I'm sorry," Holly said. "Sorry about your friend."

"Yeah." Petunia tightened her lips. "Me too." She gave Holly a kind look. "But if there's anyone who will know what to do about your brother, it's Marco. Trust me."

"OK," Holly said. She could certainly use the help. Still, the thought of Hector alone in the woods by himself ate at her. "It's just that he's younger. And . . . impulsive."

All around them, evening was blending into night, the contours of the trees merging with shadow. Night life began to stir in scattered scratches and calls.

"Hey," Petunia said, putting a reassuring hand on Holly's shoulder. "We're OK. *It* always runs after the gray boy, if she hears him. He's always laughing or singing or something. Kid is nuts, if you ask me."

"Who is he?" Holly asked.

"Better if we talk later." Petunia squinted at the tree-tops. "Just in case. But don't worry. We're almost there."

They came to a stop at a small ridge bulging from the ground in a rugged hump. Moss speckled the rocks, and the surrounding trees had blanketed the area in thick piles of fallen leaves.

"Home sweet home," Petunia said, looking satisfied.

Holly spun around, wondering what she had missed. "I don't see anything."

Petunia gave Holly a firm but lighthearted pat on the back. "Watch." She stooped down next to the ridge and began fussing with the leaves. Then she lay on her belly, turning to face Holly. Her legs slid away, disappearing. She smiled and waved, and then the rest of her dropped out of sight.

Holly rushed over to the ridge. Only up close, behind the piles of leaves, could she see it. A small opening where the ridge met the ground. A hole just big enough for a kid to slide into.

"Hurry up!" Petunia's muted voice came from below.

Holly peered into the hole. It was too dark to see anything inside.

"Just drop down!" she heard Petunia say beneath her.

Holly got on her belly, just as she'd seen Petunia do, and slid her feet into the hole. She didn't feel anything below to rest her feet on, just empty space.

"Don't worry. It's not far," Petunia said.

Holly felt a hand on her foot. Relieved, she lowered herself all the way into the opening and let go. Her feet hit the ground almost immediately.

Petunia smirked. "Not a bad hiding place, right? C'mon."

Barely any light fell from the cave entrance above. All Holly could see was that the space was narrow. Petunia moved deeper into the cave, and Holly followed, keeping her hand on the wall and feeling her way forward.

Soon the narrow passage opened up. Holly could tell they'd entered a larger space, but she couldn't see anything. Petunia moved away from her, leaving Holly stranded in the dark.

"Petunia?" Holly called to her. "You still there?"

In answer, a light clicked on. Petunia was a few feet in front of her, holding a small flashlight, about the size of a marker.

"Lucky I had this on me when I hopped on that oxcart," Petunia said. "Can't keep it on too long, though. Gotta save the batteries."

Petunia shined the light around, letting Holly see the contours of the cave. They were in a spacious area, about the size of her living room back home. Rocks large and small covered the interior, and some big slabs jutted from the ground like crags on a mountain. Walking around in the dark would be treacherous. Petunia didn't keep the light in one place for long, but Holly thought she noticed a pile of something—clothes or supplies of some kind—against one wall.

"Not much to it," Petunia said. "But it's safe. Someplace we can sleep, catch our breath." She frowned. "Marco's not here, though. Thought he'd be back by now."

From above came the faint sound of branches and leaves rustling under gusts of wind. The wind must have been fierce for Holly to hear it underground. A rumbling sound followed, like the sky clearing its throat. Thunder.

Petunia motioned for Holly to follow her. "Come on, you should see this."

Petunia led her deeper into the cave. Holly wondered how far back it went. They stepped over jagged rocks, climbing them like stairs, until they got to a section where the walls of the cave narrowed again, forming a thin crevice that was too tight to squeeze through.

"Dead end?" Holly asked.

Petunia shook her head and shined the flashlight above them. The light settled on a smooth upper part of the cave wall. Something colorful was scrawled all across the rock. It almost looked like graffiti.

Holly went over to take a closer look.

There were words. Messages. They were written in chalk, mostly in white, but some in other shades like red or blue or green. There were so many, all crammed next to each other like the back page of a yearbook.

Some were simple, like *John was here,* or just a name

and date, like *Mary Jane Portnoy, July 1975.* Others were desperate calls to home: *Remember me. I miss you, Mom and Dad. Find me.* Holly felt a tug of sorrow when she read those.

But other messages grabbed her attention. They seemed to be advice, hints and clues that others had learned about this place. *Beware red eyes. If it rains, get out! Do not travel at night. A river is to the west.* A few sentences were circled. *Don't trust Oliver. Blueberries good, red berries BAD. The gray boy knows the way.*

She stopped at that last one. She recalled the boy with gray hair, hiding behind the statue. The boy Max had chased after.

"The gray boy?" Holly asked Petunia. "The one from the field?"

"His name's Edmond," Petunia said. She sighed. "He used to help us."

"Used to?" Holly frowned, confused. "What do you mean?"

"He found us when we first got here," Petunia said. "Led us to this cave, taught us how to hide from *It.* Said he'd been here longer than anyone, that he could take us *home.*" Petunia shrugged. "And then one day, he left."

"But why?" Holly asked, unable to hide the urgency and hope in her voice. This Edmond kid knew how to get home. Why wouldn't he help them?

"That's the craziest thing." Petunia scoffed. "He said he wasn't having any *fun.*"

Her answer left Holly speechless. That anyone could think this was fun, could treat it like an actual game, was unfathomable.

Wind and thunder shook the forest outside again. It was beginning to rain.

"Hey." Holly pointed to the writing on the wall. "What about that message? *If it rains, get out!*"

"Oh, don't worry," Petunia said. "It's rained before. Nothing happened. Besides, we can gather some rainwater."

Just then, there was a thump behind them, like something heavy hitting the ground.

"Petunia? Max?" a boy's voice called in the dark.

A wave of relief crossed Petunia's face, followed quickly by a look of profound sadness.

"Let me tell him about Max, OK?" Petunia whispered. She went back toward the cave entrance. Holly followed.

"I didn't find anyone," the boy, who had to be Marco, said. "Can only hope they got lucky and found one of the old hiding spots." He sounded frustrated.

Petunia ran ahead, leaving Holly to feel her way through the shadows, trailing the glow from the flashlight. The light stopped moving. Two figures were huddled in front of her, but Holly could just make out their silhouettes.

"Marco," Petunia said, her voice wavering.

"Where's Max?"

She shook her head.

"Petunia? Where's Max?" Marco said again. It was more like a demand than a question.

"He didn't make it," Petunia said. "I'm sorry."

Marco covered his mouth. He took a breath, inhaling slowly, like it was a great effort. His hand was shaking. Petunia touched his shoulder, trying to comfort him.

"It was Edmond, wasn't it?" Marco said. "Tell me what happened." He rubbed his eyes, then abruptly stopped. "Wait." He'd finally noticed Holly standing apart from them, deeper in the cave. "Who's that?"

"Oh," Petunia said. "I did find someone out there. Holly, come over here."

Holly went to them. Petunia shined the flashlight on her.

"Marco, this is Holly," Petunia said. "Holly, this is Marco."

The light shone on Marco. He had tan skin and brown hair and dark eyes and a small mole on his right cheek. He looked exactly like Max.

He also looked to be in shock.

"Holly?" His voice was hot with emotion and confusion. He grabbed her, squeezing her shoulders, speaking with what inexplicably sounded like recognition. "What are you *doing* here?"

12

"FIRST WE MUST HIDE," EDMOND SAID, HIS GRAY EYES WIDE AND serious. "She always pursues new arrivals with extra vigor."

Hector didn't fully understand what Edmond was saying, but he nodded anyway.

This kid with the gray hair and eyes was very strange. He had started things off by jumping out of nowhere and tackling Hector, which had startled him and honestly kind of hurt. His hands and knees were still a little sore. Asking Hector if he wanted to play was super weird too. But Hector had put all of that aside and asked Edmond the one thing he needed to know: "Can you help me?"

Edmond had said yes.

Now they were crouched beneath a tree. Through the leaves above, Hector could see dark storm clouds gathering. The wind blew, and the forest shivered around them. Somewhere, the wolf howled again.

"See?" Edmond raised his eyebrows. He seemed

excited. "There she is. Quickly. Come this way." Edmond turned and strode into the forest, leaving Hector no choice but to follow.

Edmond certainly looked like he knew his way around. He slipped through the woods quietly but with confidence, seeming to know right when and where to turn and adjust his path. He did this even though it wasn't easy to see. With the clouds and setting sun, it was getting darker with each passing minute.

Edmond stopped. He stood in front of a pile of leaves and branches near the trunk of a fallen tree.

"Why did we stop?" Hector asked.

Edmond moved the branches aside, revealing a shallow pit in the ground. He smiled at Hector and hopped into the hole.

Hector peered down. Edmond was squatting in the little trench. He motioned for Hector to join him.

Of course, Hector remembered. *We're playing hide-and-seek. And this is a place to hide.*

He hopped down with Edmond, who reached up and pulled the branches back to cover the opening. It was dark and cramped in the hole, but a little bit of light broke through the gaps in the leaves.

They sat, silent and motionless. Minutes passed.

Being wedged in there with Edmond reminded Hector of the way he and Holly used to lie next to each other, scrunched up in the same bed. He would come into her room at night, back when he got scared. Instead of sleeping, they'd stay up playing stupid games, like the one where Holly would say a word and Hector had to rhyme with it.

Ring.

Fling.

Wring.

You already said that!

Different ring. Wah-ring.

Ugh. Nerd. Fine. Intergalactic smuggling ring.

That's just ring!

Nope! Different ring! I win.

Bin.

They'd keep going until Mom and Dad heard them laughing.

That was a long time ago, though.

Edmond took a quick breath and nudged Hector. Something was moving aboveground. Something on four legs. Something with heavy paws.

The wolf. Probably the same one that was chasing Holly, Hector thought. He hoped she had been able to get away.

Hector heard sniffing, and the gravelly rumble of the wolf's growl. Beside him, Edmond had a look of barely contained glee on his face, as if this whole thing were completely hilarious.

More sounds came from above. The wolf was treading

slowly. Grass and leaves crunched with each step. The sounds were fading. The wolf was moving away from them.

"Cheep!"

Hector snapped his head toward Edmond. Had he just cheeped, of all things?

"Cheep!" Edmond looked right at Hector while he did it again. Edmond was giggling.

Above, all was quiet. Hector imagined the wolf standing still, its ears perked, waiting to pounce in their direction. He couldn't begin to guess why Edmond was making noise. He was giving them away!

Unless he knows something I don't, Hector thought. Edmond had known where this hiding spot was, after all. And he had asked Hector if he wanted to *play.* Maybe that was what he was *supposed* to do.

It was worth a shot.

"Meep!" Hector squeaked. He laughed a little too.

Edmond's eyes bulged in delighted surprise. He put his hand over his mouth, trying and failing to contain his laughter.

A shadow fell on the branches overhead. The shadow's form shifted in strange ways, like it was getting longer, thinner. It sounded like something was stretching.

A branch moved. Long, pale fingers poked through the leaves, curling, ready to grasp.

Then, from somewhere nearby, came a low, steady

whistle. The hand paused. The tone gradually changed pitch, each note blending into the next. It was a song, a simple, somber melody.

The pale hand drew back. Then came more peculiar sounds. Hector swore he could hear feathers ruffling and spreading. A bird screeched, its call fading as it flew away.

Edmond popped to his feet. He pushed the foliage out of the way and heaved himself out of the hole.

Hector got up to follow. He put his hands on the edge and tried pulling himself up. It took him a couple of tries. Edmond stared down at him, waiting.

Finally, Hector managed to haul himself out. He dusted off his clothes.

The sun was almost down. The clouds above rumbled. It would be completely dark soon.

"This way," Edmond said. He turned his back on Hector and proceeded into the woods.

"Hey!" Hector ran after him. He dashed ahead and stood in Edmond's way, forcing him to stop.

"Can you tell me what's going on here?" Hector asked. "Where are we? What is this place?"

"Oh, let me guess." Edmond dramatically covered his eyes with his hands and threw his head back. "You want to go *home*. Home, home, home. It's all *anybody* wants!"

"No," Hector said. "I want to find my sister."

Edmond dropped his hands. "What?"

"My sister," Hector repeated. "Holly. She's here. I need

to find her."

Edmond stroked his chin. "*We'd* be the ones seeking." He grinned at Hector. "I *like* this game!"

A wet drop splattered on Hector's arm, then on his neck.

"It's raining," Hector said, looking up.

"That's OK," Edmond said. "I know a place."

"Not another hole in the ground."

"How did you know?" Edmond laughed. "It's not just a hole, though." Edmond raised his eyebrows. "You'll like it. It's a cave."

13

IT WAS HARD FOR HOLLY TO FALL ASLEEP.

Marco had recognized her. She was sure of it. Just like his twin brother, Max, had back in the woods.

When Marco noticed Holly's confused reaction, he had quickly made excuses: *Sorry, case of mistaken identity. You remind me of someone else.* But when she told him that Hector was here too, his eyes practically popped out of his head.

Holly had wanted to go search for him right away, but Marco and Petunia both insisted that it was too dangerous to search at night. They gave her some food—a palmful of tiny nuts and some small, mushy berries—and brought her to a bed of leaves to rest.

Holly tried to sleep, but her mind swirled, her thoughts and memories and feelings spinning like a hurricane in a jar. She thought of her mom and dad. What would they be doing at home, all alone? Still looking for something they couldn't find? She thought of Hector. *He's going to be OK,* she told herself. *I'm going to find him.*

Finally, Holly dreamt.

She was in her room back home, but it was all wrong. Her room was always tidy, with everything in its proper place, but now it was a mess. Her books were strewn across the floor, like someone had come in and tossed them haphazardly from their spots on the shelf. Probably Hector. She would have to reorganize everything. Alphabetically by author, of course. She scanned the covers, looking for last names that began with an *A*.

Hector came in. This was expected. He always came to her room when he couldn't sleep. In the twisted logic of the dream, Holly just accepted that it was night now, and it was totally normal that she was suddenly in her pajamas. Rain pattered against her window.

"I can't sleep," Hector said, rubbing his eyes.

"Why'd you mess up my books?" she grumbled.

Hector sat down next to her. She made room for him. He had paper and a pencil.

"Let's play," he said. He picked up the pencil and drew a curly line. Then he handed the pencil to Holly.

This was a game of theirs. One of them would start with a random scribble. The other would have to add to it, trying to make it into something recognizable. Then they'd take turns until their picture was complete.

Hector's scribbled line looked a little like one half of a villain's mustache that curled at the ends. Holly drew the other side of the mustache, a nose, and some eyes. She handed Hector the pencil.

"Hmph," he said. He drew a rectangle around the face and added a little handle on top. "Mr. Suitcase Head."

Holly couldn't help but laugh. "That's so dumb." But her mind was already racing to top his absurdity. Maybe she'd give him octopus legs. "Here, my turn."

Hector ignored her, continuing to draw. Outside, the rain picked up. It was really coming down.

"Hey, come on, my turn," she said again, reaching for the pencil.

Hector didn't acknowledge her in any way. She tried to grab the pencil, but it wouldn't budge.

"Hello? Hector?" she said. He said nothing. "Hector!"

She was starting to get desperate. She stood. She shouted his name. She shoved him and pulled on him, and still he wouldn't respond. A voice deep in her mind began repeating, *Not again, not again. I can't do this again.*

Thunder clapped, rattling the whole house. And just like that, Hector turned on her. He grabbed her by the shoulders and started shaking her.

"Wake up!" he shouted. He wouldn't stop shaking her. "Holly, wake up!"

Holly opened her eyes. It wasn't Hector shaking her, but Marco. He had the flashlight. He was shining the flashlight right in her face.

"Turn it off." She squinted and held her hand out to block the light. She shifted away from Marco, and her legs splashed cold water.

Wait, Holly thought. *Why are my legs in water?*

"The cave is flooding," Marco said. He grabbed Holly's hand and pulled her up. She realized she was soaked.

Marco yanked on her arm, pulling her with him as he hurried across the cave. Holly stumbled after him, water sloshing around her calves. The cave was filling up fast.

They reached the cave entrance, where Petunia was waiting. The small opening was just overhead. Rain pelted the rock, while flashes of lightning lit up the night.

"We have to climb out," Marco shouted over the storm. "Holly, you first! Wait at the top!"

Before she could even respond, Marco grabbed her and lifted her up. She grasped at the slippery, wet rock and squirmed her way out. Next came Petunia.

"Help me with Marco," Petunia said. They turned back to the hole and reached down, clutching Marco by the arms, pulling him out of the cave.

The downpour drenched them. They scurried together to a nearby tree, huddling by the trunk. The canopy of leaves overhead blocked some of the rain.

"I thought you said it had rained before," Holly said.

"Yeah, well, not like this," said Marco. "I think we can stay here until the rain lets up." He folded his arms tight against his chest, shivering. "Let's just hope it doesn't take the cave too long to drain."

Gusts of wind blew water sideways into their meager shelter by the tree. It felt like the sky was attacking them. Rain shot down in unceasing, rapid-fire bursts, while volleys of thunder and lightning detonated in the clouds.

With the lightning illuminating the night, Holly could just make out the outline of bushes trembling, of tree limbs creaking and bending to the will of the storm.

There was another flash of lightning. Ahead, through the haze of rain, Holly could have sworn she saw the silhouette of someone huddled under a tree.

Hector?

Without hesitating, she ran toward him.

"Hector!" she cried. He didn't move.

She got to the tree and stumbled down to her knees. His back was to her, his body crouched like a beetle rolled up into a ball.

"Hector!" she said once more, but still he didn't move.

She put a hand on his back. It was coarse and solid. It was made of stone.

No.

She crawled around to the front of the statue. It was too

dark to see much detail, so she ran her hands over the face and head.

The head was smooth and round. It didn't feel at all like hair. There was a little raised button in the middle, and a long bill over the forehead. It was a hat. Holly breathed a sigh of relief.

Hector wasn't wearing a hat.

Then the eyes of the statue flashed red, sparking like flame.

Holly jumped back. She half expected the statue to come to life and start chasing her, but it remained motionless. Its eyes glowed for another second, then went out, returning to stone.

Marco and Petunia came up behind her, concern all over their faces.

"I thought . . ." Holly started. "Never mind. It's not Hector."

"Don't run off like that!" Marco said. "Ever! Do you know what—"

He was cut off by a howl.

They turned to see something in the distance. Something low to the ground, making slow, deliberate movements. Something with red eyes.

"Run," Marco whispered.

They ran. Holly picked herself up and stumbled forward, her foot squishing into muddy terrain. She felt a hand on her shoulder, grasping at her shirt.

"Stay together," Marco said.

Holly reached behind, found Petunia's arm, and took it. Marco grabbed Holly's other hand. The three of them tromped forward in the dark, clinging to one another, Marco leading the way.

Between the darkness and the storm and the rain pelting her face, Holly could barely see anything ahead besides the shape of Petunia's back. She looked behind her, and the red eyes were still there. They seemed larger, closer. While the three of them were practically walking blind, *It* could probably see everything.

"This way!" Marco called from up front. "To the stream. If we cross, maybe we can lose *It*."

Crossing a stream? Would that work? Could Marco even tell where they were going? Holly didn't know, but she also didn't have any better ideas. She followed, planting one foot after another into the slippery mud. Each step was a struggle to stay upright, and more than once she had to grasp on to Petunia to keep from falling, almost knocking them both over.

Strands of wet hair stuck to her forehead and cheeks. Her braid was coming apart. Holly became aware of a new sound, something other than the drum of rain and wind and the cymbal crash of thunder. This sound was a wet, rushing roar, the sound of water flowing with storm-whipped speed.

It had to be the stream Marco was talking about. But

it didn't sound nearly gentle enough to be called a mere *stream*. This sounded like flooding waters that had just burst from a dam.

"Uh-oh," Marco said. "Stop!"

"Watch out!" Petunia cried.

Holly tried to stop. But it was too late.

14

HOLLY CRASHED INTO PETUNIA. THE GROUND GAVE WAY. THE sloppy mud squished beneath her feet, and suddenly she was on her back, skidding down, unable to slow herself. She slid faster and faster, Marco and Petunia shouting beside her, all of them plummeting helplessly like debris in an avalanche until their fall ended in a piercing cold splash.

It was the river.

As soon as Holly hit the water, she sank, her momentum plunging her below. The current grabbed her, pulling her, carrying her away.

The river had her and wasn't letting go.

Her first thought was that she was going to drown. She was submerged, at the mercy of fierce rushing waves that pummeled and swept her helpless body forward.

But her second thought was angry and emphatic: *No, I will not.*

She was *not* helpless, she told herself. She knew what to do.

Don't panic. Don't thrash about. Don't fight the current. Swim with it.

She extended her arms and started to kick. She angled up, trying to rise. The river fought her, pummeling her with unpredictable waves. She churned her legs, reaching and pulling with her hands. She had one thought, one goal, and she wasn't going to be stopped.

Holly broke through to the surface. She opened her mouth and took hungry gasps of air. She had done it.

Moonlight shone through parting clouds. The rain was letting up.

"Petunia?" she called out. There was no response. She wanted to call out to Marco, but the river pushed her forward, dragging her, slapping water in her face. It was difficult to keep her head above water.

"Holly?" Marco yelled. "Where are you?"

In the water, same as you, she thought. That wasn't helpful, though. She twisted her neck and tried to look around—the moonlight was making it slightly easier to see—but she couldn't find anyone else. All she saw was a dark shape looming ahead, getting closer as the river rushed her toward it.

The dark shape was a rock, Holly realized. It split the river. To the right, the river continued to flow. To the left, it looked like the water came to an end, lapping up against a shoreline piled with branches and debris.

"To the left!" Holly shouted. "Swim to the left!"

Holly kept herself aloft, kicking and stroking toward the riverbank. She could only hope that Marco and Petunia had heard her.

"Left!" she yelled again.

"Go left!" Marco repeated from behind. "Follow Holly!"

She surged past the rock. The riverbank was coming up fast. She careened toward the sharp jumble of broken tree limbs and soaking, dead leaves.

To protect her face, Holly shifted her weight and floated on her back, putting her feet forward, preparing to let her legs take the brunt of the inevitable crash.

The river washed her into the debris. Tree limbs snapped, and branches clawed at her legs. Her feet hit something solid, and Holly immediately pushed back, like she was kicking off at the edge of a pool. It worked to slow her momentum, and she was able to put her feet down.

She could stand.

She pushed and tossed branches out of her way, her legs slogging through the mucky water. At last she was able to raise her foot and plant it on solid ground. She stumbled onto land, falling to her knees, her fingers sinking into the soft mud.

She had made it.

15

HECTOR JOURNEYED INTO THE WOODS WITH EDMOND IN the dark and rain and wind. Edmond was an expert guide, or at least he seemed to be. They crept and picked their way through the forest, Edmond stopping every now and then to touch a tree or perk his head up and listen. Then they'd shift direction and keep going.

More than once Edmond turned back to Hector to tell him to keep up. It was just like Holly telling him what to do.

She probably walked through the forest perfectly, he thought, rolling his eyes.

Then he remembered Holly's face back at the park, red from crying.

I'm going to find her, he told himself. *I'm going to make this right.*

"Hey," Hector called over to Edmond. "Is this really hide-and-seek?"

Edmond stopped and squatted down. Raindrops splattered on his head.

"Do you wish to converse for a moment?" he asked. "Before we continue our trek?"

"Yeah," Hector said, kneeling beside him. "Let's converse."

"What queries do you have?"

"Do you always talk like that?" Hector asked. Edmond didn't respond. Hector wished he could see his expression, but it was too dark. "Never mind. I was asking if we're really playing hide-and-seek."

"The Hiddenseek," Edmond corrected him.

"Yeah, but that's just another name for hide-and-seek, right? Like, someone's *It* and they're trying to catch us? Is *It* that wolf?"

"Sometimes."

"Oh." Hector nodded, as if that made any sense. "So how do we win?"

"Win?" Edmond asked, like the concept was foreign to him.

"There's a way to win, right?" Hector edged closer to Edmond. "To get back home?"

Edmond scowled. "There it is, what everybody wants. *Home, home, home.* I thought we were seeking your sister."

"We are, but do you know where it is? The way home?"

Edmond crossed his arms and turned his head from Hector, but he nodded. *"Yes."*

"So why are you still here?"

Again, Hector was met with silence.

Thunder cracked, and what had been spitting rain became an unrelenting downpour. It had been hard to see before. Now it was impossible.

"The cave is near," Edmond said. "Your sister will be there. If she has not already been caught."

"Why didn't you say so!" Hector exclaimed. That was the best news he'd heard yet.

"Grab ahold of my shirt," Edmond said. "Don't let go."

Hector did as he was told and grasped Edmond's soaking-wet shirt. Then Edmond took off. Hector lurched forward, his feet skidding over the muddy forest floor to keep up.

Edmond moved fast. It was like the rain and the dark didn't slow him down at all. Hector tried once or twice to talk to him again, but he never responded. The only sound was the pounding roar of the storm.

Suddenly, Edmond stopped. Hector collided with him.

"What on earth—" Hector said.

In front of them was a giant mass of fog. It rolled and pulsed, expanding and contracting, almost like it was a breathing, living thing.

Edmond drew back. "We can't go this way."

"What is it?" Hector asked.

But Edmond just turned and ran.

"Edmond?" Hector called for him. "Edmond!"

And just like that, Hector was alone.

He took one more look at the strange fog and then chased after Edmond into the black, dark forest.

He stumbled about blindly, frantically searching the shadows for any sign of Edmond. He called his name, but there was no response. He dashed forward every time he saw a hint of movement in the dark or heard the snapping of branches. Every time he found nothing. He spun around and realized he had no idea where that weird fog was now, where he was, where anything was. He was completely, utterly lost and on his own.

"Oof!" The yelp came from somewhere on Hector's left. It sounded like someone falling.

"Help!" Edmond's voice carried over the storm. "Help!"

Hector ran toward the cries. He skidded to a stop at a steep, muddy embankment. He heard the sound of rushing water and could just make out the dark ripples of a flowing river below.

Right in front of him, clinging to the side of the ridge, was Edmond. His fingers were sinking into the mud, slipping.

Hector reached down and grabbed Edmond's hands. They were freezing, like he'd just dipped his hands in a bucket of ice. They were so cold it hurt, and every instinct in his body told Hector to let go. But he ignored the pain and the cold and held on tighter. He heaved with all his might and pulled Edmond up.

Edmond and Hector both toppled over onto the ground. They sat in the mud, panting.

"You caught me," Edmond said. He seemed to be in disbelief. "You saved me."

Moonlight pushed through the clouds. The rain was finally letting up. Hector was so exhausted he could only nod. Edmond just continued to stare at him, his eyes welling with gratitude.

They both turned their heads back down to the river at a new sound. Someone was yelling. Actually, more than one person. They were calling names out as the river carried them away.

"Petunia!"

"Holly!"

Hector turned to Edmond. "It's Holly! My sister!" Hector got up, trying to see where the river led. He reached down and pulled Edmond to his feet. "Come on! We've got to go find her."

16

HOLLY WAS SAFELY OUT OF THE RIVER, BUT THERE WAS NO TIME to relax.

Marco came barreling downstream past the rock and smashed into the mound of debris with a painful-sounding crunch.

Holly rushed to where he stood tangled in the branches and flotsam. He had a cut on his face, just above the eye. It was bleeding. He coughed violently, spitting water out of his mouth.

"You OK?" she asked. "Where's Petunia?"

"Behind me," Marco said, thumbing backward. "See if you can help her."

Holly left Marco to extract himself from the river. The storm seemed to have passed. There was only a light drizzle now, and the absence of trees overhead offered an un-encumbered view. Clouds parted, revealing a sky strewn with stars. But all she saw in the river was rushing water and a floating piece of driftwood, one of its branches swaying back and forth in the wind.

Then Holly looked again. That wasn't a swaying branch. It was an arm. It was waving.

Petunia had grabbed a log and was using it to stay afloat. But she wasn't floating the right way. She was heading straight for the rock.

Holly shouted to her, "This way!"

She saw Petunia's head disappear underwater. A sudden fear gripped Holly. *What if she can't swim?*

Then she saw Petunia's colorful hair break the surface of the water, bobbing up and down. *She's walking,* Holly realized, relieved.

Finally, Petunia reached the edge, the water coming up only to her knees now. Holly held out a hand, helping her onto the shore.

"Thanks," Petunia said. She put her hands on her knees, catching her breath.

Marco joined them. Everyone was drenched, their clothes heavy and dripping. The cut above Marco's eye wasn't bleeding anymore, but it had left a long red streak on his forehead.

"No idea where we are." Marco peered upriver in the direction they'd come from. "No telling how far we are from the cave." He looked to the sky. Clouds were rolling back in, shrouding the stars, threatening more rain.

Holly wasn't concerned about the weather, though.

How far was she from Hector now? Would she ever find him?

"We can't stay out in the open," Petunia said.

Marco nodded. "We have to move."

Everyone gathered themselves. Holly squeezed her hair, wringing out water and hoping to leave the ordeal in the river behind. There was no time to dwell on it.

They walked near one another, taking careful steps away from the river. They had come to the edge of the woods. The trees here were shorter, all flat-leafed. The ground was clear of brush. Somewhere in the distance, Holly thought she heard something else moving behind them, back in the thick of the forest. They couldn't afford to linger.

"Look." Holly pointed. It was still difficult to see, but she could just make out a line where the grass gave way to a trail of dirt. "I think this is a path."

Marco and Petunia agreed. A path meant someone else, at some time, had been here. It was a sign of something other than endless wilderness.

They followed the trail. It curved into the woods, but the trees here were sparse. Soon they emerged into a small clearing.

There was a building nestled between the trees. It was tall, with a sharp steeple on top. There was a circular window on the second story, and narrow stairs led to two large wooden doors up front.

It was a church.

"Whoa," Marco said. "I thought everything here was forest."

Petunia stepped forward, but Holly quickly grabbed her by the shoulder.

"Wait!" Holly pulled her back.

In front of the church, just off to the side, was a statue. A girl, sitting cross-legged, her head down. It was the first statue Holly had seen where the kid didn't look scared. This one looked like she had just . . . given up.

"Walk *behind* the statue," Holly said.

"Huh?" Petunia looked at Holly like she'd grown another nose. "Why?"

"Yeah." Marco sounded interested. "Why?"

It was something that had been working in the back of Holly's mind. She had first noticed it when Max ran into the field after Edmond. And later at the statue outside the cave.

"The eyes," Holly said. "When someone passes in front of a statue, its eyes turn red. Just like the eyes on *It*. I think it's like an alarm or something."

Marco and Petunia looked at each other.

"What do you think?" he asked her.

"I think she's a genius." Petunia chuckled. "Or we're idiots."

"Or a little of both." Marco grinned.

"I mean, think about it." Petunia slapped him on the back. "That's why no one could ever cross the big field."

"Yeah . . ." His smile faded. He was obviously thinking of his brother.

"Oh, Marco, I'm sorry," Petunia said.

"Forget it," he said. "Let's get inside. But *around* the statue." He patted Holly on the shoulder. "Good job, Hollister."

Holly felt something weird, like déjà vu, from being called Hollister. No one called her that. She was sure of it. But somehow it felt familiar. It felt right.

Suddenly, she remembered what Oliver had said, that everyone who knew her would forget her. The same thing must be true for Marco. For everyone brought to the Hiddenseek. *Anyone who knew him would forget he existed,* Holly realized. *Including me.*

Petunia began making her way to the far side of the clearing, away from the statue. Marco moved to follow, but Holly grabbed him by the arm.

"Wait," Holly said. "Did I know you? From before? Is that why you know who I am, but I don't remember you?"

"Should've known you'd figure it out." Marco smiled at her. "You do know me, Holly. I'm your older brother."

Holly's mouth dropped open.

"Actually, *oldest* brother," Marco said, his voice going soft. "Max . . . he was a minute behind me."

It was impossible. How could she have no memory of a brother? Of *twin* brothers?

"What are you two waiting for?" Petunia called back to them.

"I promise," Marco said, "there's nothing I want more than to talk about this. But let's get inside where it's safe first."

He motioned for Holly to follow him. She nodded. She was numb with shock.

He looks like Mom, Holly realized. How had she not seen that before? She pictured her mom rummaging through the closet, looking for something she could never find. *That's what she was missing. Her sons.*

They joined Petunia, making sure to stay out of the statue's line of sight. Once far enough past the statue, they doubled back and finally arrived at the front of the church. They climbed the short wooden stairs, which groaned under their feet, and approached the big wooden doors.

"Should we knock?" Petunia asked.

"C'mon," Marco said, reaching for the door. "Who would be way out here?"

But before Marco could close his grip around the handle, the door moved. It swung open, forcing him backward.

Someone was already there.

17

HOLLY JUMPED BACK. TWO BOYS STOOD IN THE DOORWAY OF the church.

"The statue!" one boy said, panic in his voice. He was short and pale, with a pair of smudged glasses, a matted head of black hair, and a black T-shirt. "Did you step in front of the statue?"

"No," Holly said. "We went around."

He raised his eyebrows. "You guys figured it out?" He sounded impressed.

"She did." Petunia put a hand on Holly's shoulder. "Can we come inside now?"

The other boy came forward. He was taller, with long brown hair down to his shoulders. He wore a yellow-and-red soccer jersey and a confident smirk on his face. He was also holding something that looked like a net bunched up in his hands. "George, don't be rude," he said.

"But you—" George began, but the other boy cut him off.

"Please, all of you, come in."

They entered the church together and gathered in the front. Holly felt relieved to step inside an actual structure, to not be in the wilderness and exposed to the elements.

The interior of the church was austere. Symmetrical rows of pews were separated by a long center aisle. The walls were bare except for a series of arched windows on each side, their glass smudged by dirt and grime. The floor panels creaked under their weight. At the far end of the church was a simple wooden altar. Two flickering candles rested there, providing light.

The boy in the soccer jersey slid into a pew, flinging his net down beside him. He leaned back and propped his feet up. "Welcome to our dreary, terrible home." He gestured around him. "I'm Javier."

They all took turns introducing themselves.

Javier snapped his fingers when they were done. "Make yourselves at home," he said. "We were *trying* to sleep when we heard you outside."

Petunia plopped down on one of the pews. Holly stood in the aisle next to George.

Marco, though, was all business. "Mind if I take a look around?" he asked.

Javier shrugged, and Marco began walking around the perimeter of the church.

"You guys hungry?" George asked. "Or thirsty? We have apples. There's an orchard nearby. And we get water from the river . . ."

"Can't see through the windows," Marco said. It sounded like he was talking to himself. "That's good."

"You guys are the first other kids we've seen. How long have you been here?" George asked Holly.

"They've been here awhile," Holly answered, nodding toward Marco and Petunia. "I just got here today."

"*Today?*" George spat. "Wow. You're really holding it together. I was a wreck my first day."

"Thanks," Holly said. "I guess. What about you?"

"Four months," George said. "Javier arrived about a day after me. Been together ever since."

"*Four months,*" Holly repeated. It was her turn to be surprised. And scared. That was a long time to be here without finding the way home.

"One quick thing," Javier said. He abruptly brushed past Marco, bumping shoulders with him, then walked to the front door. He went into his back pocket and pulled out a large metal key. It was the size of a screwdriver, browned by rust and age, with a decorative oval ring on top and two thick bits protruding like teeth from the end.

"My key. My church." Javier stuck the key in the door and turned. The lock slid into place with a heavy clunk.

"You are, of course, welcome to stay." He bowed. "As long as you do what you're told."

Holly turned to George. "Is he serious?"

George looked away, embarrassed.

"It's fine," Marco said.

"It is?" Petunia scoffed.

"We're tired. *I'm* tired," Marco said. "We're happy to abide by your rules. We're just grateful for the help."

Javier nodded and returned to his spot in the pew.

Marco came over to Holly. "We'll go out and look for Hector as soon as it's light. For now, we should sleep." He patted her on the shoulder and took a seat on the opposite side of the aisle.

"George?" Javier snapped his fingers twice in quick succession. "The lights?"

The candles on the altar each had a simple brass base with a wide brim to catch the wax. Between them, at the center of the altar, was a Bible.

George reached for the first candle, but Holly put a hand on his arm to stop him.

"Is this real?" Holly asked, pointing to the Bible. The cracked and worn leather on the cover of the thick volume looked ancient.

George nodded. There was an excited glint to his eyes. "Open it," he urged her.

Tucked inside the front cover was a folded-up letter. Opposite that was the title page. It was bordered by a series of small, ornate drawings, each in its own little box. At the center of the page was a heart, inside of which the title and inscription were written.

"Look." George pointed to the bottom of the inscription. It read

OXFORD:

Printed by JOHN BASKETT,

printer to the King's most Excellent Majesty,

and the University.

MDCCXV.

Holly quickly deciphered the roman numerals. "1715."

"Yep," George said in a secretive whisper, "I think *every-thing* here is that old. Open that letter. I found it in the back." He pointed to a door behind the altar.

Holly touched the Bible's paper. It was yellowed but thin and smooth. Something on the inside cover, though, caught her eye. It was written in cursive handwriting:

Covenant Church

"What's that?" Holly pointed to the writing.

"It's exactly what you think it is," George said. "Go on. Open the letter."

"Are you having trouble with the candles, George?" Javier grumbled from the back of the church.

"Ignore him," Holly said. Her hands were shaking. "George, where are you from?"

"Covenant." He gave Holly a knowing look. "And where are you from?"

From his expression, Holly could tell he already knew the answer. "Marco! Petunia!" she shouted.

Marco and Petunia sat up, their eyes sleepy but curious.

Javier slapped his hand on the pew. "Lights!" he moaned. "I said turn out the lights! Why can't you understand lights?" He turned to Marco. "Why can't she understand lights?"

"What is it, Holly?" Marco ignored Javier. "What's so important?"

Holly smiled. "I know where we are."

18

HOLLY STRODE DOWN THE AISLE. SHE APPROACHED JAVIER FIRST, who was eyeing her with unconcealed skepticism.

"Where are you from?" she asked him. "What town?"

"Ugh." He shook his head. "You're as bad as George with this nonsense."

"Is it Covenant?"

"Yes!" Javier clapped his hands in mock celebration. "Well done! We're all from the same crappy town. Can I go to sleep now?"

"It's not that we're all *from* Covenant," Holly explained. "We're all *still in* Covenant."

She opened the Bible and pointed to the writing on the inside cover. Everyone scooted forward in their seats to look.

"*This* is Covenant," she said. "We never left."

"See?" George said to Javier. "I told you it was important."

Then Holly pulled the folded-up letter from the front

of the book. Like the Bible, it looked ancient. Its edges were tattered, and the years had stained it yellow and brown in spots. She began unfolding it.

"Just . . . careful," George said.

"I *know*," Holly said. It felt delicate and brittle in her hands.

She scanned the page. The writing was faded, and it was difficult to read in the dim light. She squinted, bringing the paper closer to her face.

The handwriting was so neat and elegant it was almost like a work of art. She noticed the spelling of some of the words seemed strange, but she could translate them easily enough.

"What does it say?" Petunia craned her neck to try and get a glimpse.

"I'll read it out loud," Holly said. She cleared her throat and began.

29th July, 1737
Dear Pastor Latham,

"Wait." Petunia stopped her. "It's *that* old?"

"Keep reading," George prompted her. Holly returned to the letter.

I am grateful to you, as always, for your kind and patient receipt of my tidings of woe. 'Tis only a mere month, after all, since your intervention on my behalf with Mister Mullins, and you can take satisfaction that he has, at your behest, agreed to curtail the clattering of his forge in the evening.

"You can skip this part," Javier interrupted.

"Shh. Let her finish," Petunia admonished him. "Go on, Holly."

Holly smiled her thanks at Petunia and continued.

The fault is mine, of course. I am the one now forced to live above the millinery shop. Such is my fall from grace.

I implore you, once more, to press your pious and forthright good judgment upon my brother. I am certain his heart remains as good and loyal as I knew it to be in our youth. 'Tis his wife whose influence has corrupted him and turned his thoughts against me, his own sister. I say, again, fully aware of the seriousness of the allegation, that she is a Witch. I have witnessed too many times the evidence of her nefarious craft.

She follows me, still. Even having won my eviction from my home, and seeing me greatly reduced in spirit and reputation, she hounds me. She takes the form of a raven, perching nearby. She wears the countenance of a bird, but 'tis her. I know her presence.

Holly lowered the letter. "Turning into a raven . . .
She's talking about *It*."

"Well, *writing* about *It*," George said.

"Don't be pedantic," Holly blurted out. It was something her mom always used to say to her. She felt a brief
pang of longing but went on.

*I fear for my brother. I fear for those sweet children
and their imperiled souls. I beg you to intercede on their
behalf, and on my own.*

Yours very humbly,
Abigail Martin

"Children . . ." Marco said. "Do you think she means
kids like us? Stuck in the Hiddenseek? Was this witch she's
talking about turning kids to stone way back then?"

"That's what I think," George said. "It seems like too
much of a coincidence to mean anything else."

Holly turned her eyes back to the letter, reading through
it again. She felt strange—both guilty and exhilarated—to
be reading the personal thoughts of someone from so long
ago. This woman, Abigail, seemed very desperate for help.

"She says the witch is married to her brother," Holly
said. "How could she still be around hundreds of years

later?"

"How can she turn into a wolf?" George shrugged. "How can she turn kids into statues? *She's a witch!*" He wiggled his fingers like he was casting a spell.

"It doesn't say anything about hide-and-seek." Holly frowned. It was good to have learned something, however vague, about *It*. But now she had even more questions.

"Ugh!" Javier buried his face in his hands. "Bad enough I had to listen to George talk about that stupid letter all the time."

"It's not stupid." George's face flushed red.

"Hey," Marco said to Javier, "what's your problem? Don't you *want* to figure this out? Don't you want to get home?"

"Everyone, please. You are all very new here." Javier held his hands up as if to calm them. "*Very new* to our little church. What you need to know is that this place? Right here? It's safe. Out there?" He pointed toward the door. "Not safe."

"We can't just stay in this church forever," Holly said.

"Why not?" Javier scoffed. "We have everything we need right here. Food. Apples. A river with fish. Water that we can drink. All nearby. We have a roof. A door that actually locks. And if *It* somehow makes it inside?" Javier reached down onto the pew and grabbed his net, holding it aloft like a trophy. "She gets *this*!"

Holly noticed George was suddenly very intent on

studying the floor and wouldn't meet anyone's eyes. Everyone else looked at Javier like he'd just lost his mind.

Marco turned to Petunia. "We've got to get out of here."

"Agreed," she said. "First thing in the morning."

"Go ahead." Javier waved them off. "You'll be back. If you survive. I give you thirty minutes before you come running, banging on the door."

Bang! Bang! Bang!

The front door shook.

"Did . . . one of you do that?" Javier asked.

Bang-bang-bang-bang-bang!

The door rattled again, the knocks coming quicker and more frantic.

"Open up!" someone shouted from outside. "Let us in!"

Holly couldn't believe it. "Open the door," she said. "I know that voice."

19

HECTOR POUNDED HIS FIST ON THE WOODEN DOOR OF THE CHURCH.
Finally, there was a metallic click, and the door swung open. An older boy with long hair stood in the doorway.

"Let him in!" someone shouted from behind.

Holly.

Hector pushed his way past the long-haired boy and into the church. He saw her standing with a group of other kids. She was soaked from head to toe, and her clothes and hair were a mess, but it was her. His sister. He'd found her.

He ran to her and wrapped his arms around her in a big I-thought-I'd-never-see-you-again embrace.

"Hector!" she said. She sounded relieved.

"Unbelievable," another boy said. He looked older too. His hand was covering his mouth, and he actually looked like he might cry.

"We're glad to see you, little man," a girl with rainbow hair said.

"Oh." Hector eyed everyone. "Hi."

"Right," Holly said. "Everyone, this is my brother Hector." She pointed to each of the other kids in turn. "Hector, this is Petunia, Marco, George, and Javier."

There was no way Hector was going to remember all of that. He didn't care. He had found Holly. That's all that mattered.

"How did you find me?" Holly asked.

Hector pointed to Edmond, who was still standing by the front door. "I found someone who could help."

Everyone spun around. There was a sharp intake of breath from more than one person.

"That's . . ." Petunia started.

"Edmond," Marco finished.

Hector stepped closer to Marco. He seemed familiar for some reason. "You know Edmond?" Hector asked.

Edmond came forward, water dripping and pooling on the wooden floor beneath his bare feet. He eyed the rafters of the church like an owner returning from a long vacation.

"Is the rear door locked as well?" Edmond asked.

"Um . . . kinda," George answered. "Why do you ask?"

"Oh." Edmond shrugged. "Hector passed in front of the statue. I imagine we will need to exit through the back."

Holly's face turned white. Hector didn't understand. What was Edmond talking about?

"Javier!" Holly shouted. "The door! Did you lock the door?"

"Um . . ." Javier fumbled in his pockets.

The door swung open, hitting the wall with a sharp wooden crack.

A woman entered. She wore a black dress. Her long dark hair was wet and tangled and covered her face like a bramble of wild thorns.

Everyone froze in place.

The woman dripped, her chest rising and falling in deep even breaths. Her eyes glowed, giving the hair draped over her face a red tint.

Red eyes, Hector realized. *Just like the wolf.*

They needed to run. They needed to get out.

But the woman moved first.

She tossed her head back, flinging her long hair out of her eyes. She walked toward them, her steps unhurried, even elegant. She lifted a hand, not so much reaching for them but extending it, like an offer, like she expected them to take it.

George and Petunia stumbled backward. Holly grabbed ahold of Hector's arm, pulling him close. The older boy, Marco, stepped in front of them. Edmond was already at the far end of the church, slipping into a room in the back.

Javier leapt forward.

"Yargh!" he shouted. He flung his arms, tossing his net into the air. The net spread out, stretching like a spiderweb, sailing above the woman in black, and landing on her head.

The net draped over her. She tried to push it off, but one of her arms slipped through a hole, tangling her. She stumbled forward and tripped, dropping to her knees. She shook, trying to free herself, her movements becoming wild and frantic.

"That's not going to hold her for long," Holly said.

Javier grabbed one end of the net. He pulled it tight, trying to pin it to the ground.

"George!" he yelled. "George, help me!"

"Javier, don't!" George shouted. He was backing away. "Drop the stupid net!"

Marco grabbed Holly and Hector by the arm.

"We need to get out of here," he said. "Now."

"George!" Javier screamed. "Get over here! Come here and help me, you coward!"

Beneath the net, the woman in black trembled. Her convulsing was rapid and violent, like the frenzied vibration of the wings of a locust. She cast her head back, exposing her neck.

And then she shed her skin.

Her entire outer layer—skin, hair, clothes, and all—faded in color and peeled away. It was like a flower blossoming and then rotting all at once. From beneath the discarded husk of the woman emerged a snake. Its scales

105

were a glassy black, its eyes glowing red, and its fangs bared and ready to strike.

The snake slipped easily though the holes in the net.

"RUN!" Marco shouted.

But it was too late.

20

THE SNAKE COILED AND SPRANG AT JAVIER. IN MID-LUNGE IT seemed to burst apart, changing in an instant back into the woman. She landed on Javier, shoving him onto the ground. She smacked a hand down on top of his face, clutching it like she was gripping a ball.

Javier opened his mouth, but he didn't even have time to scream. His face had already turned to stone.

"NO!" George shouted.

Gray soon covered Javier's body, spreading down from his head like a slowly dripping coat of molten wax. He lay still on his back, motionless, his arms outstretched uselessly in defense. In just seconds he had become a lifeless statue, his expression stuck in a look of anguished shock.

The woman in black collapsed. She dropped to her knees, resting her head on the floor, almost like she was praying. Holly remembered she had done this before, when she turned Max to stone. Turning kids into statues took something out of her. It seemed to make her tired.

"What . . . what's happening?" Hector stammered, his eyes bulging in horror. Holly realized this must have been the first time Hector had seen the woman transform, but there was no time to explain.

"We have to go," Holly said. "We have to go *now*."

Marco began to edge around the woman in black, toward the front door. She lunged and swiped at his leg, barely missing him.

"Hector!" Edmond shouted. He was at the back of the church, behind the altar, standing in front of an open door.

It crawled forward, swiping at them again, holding her fingers out like claws. She wasn't going to let them escape out the front. Their only choice was to follow Edmond.

"Let's go!" Holly said. She pulled Hector with her as she backed away.

George stood in place, refusing to move.

Petunia went to him, clutching his arm. "You have to leave him. C'mon."

George let himself be moved, but never took his eyes off Javier.

They ran down the aisle to the room at the back of the church. Marco slammed the door shut behind them. He fumbled with the knob.

"There's no lock," he said.

The room was tiny. There was a wooden desk tucked into one corner and a wardrobe standing against the far wall. On the back wall, there was another door, presumably leading outside. A tall, empty bookshelf was propped up against it, blocking their exit.

"That bookshelf may present a problem," Edmond remarked, as if their situation were a particularly challenging puzzle and not a matter of life and death.

Marco yanked at the bookshelf, trying to move it.

"It's too heavy," he grunted.

Petunia went over to help, and the two of them pulled at the bookshelf together, their faces red with exertion.

"Everyone!" he said through gritted teeth. "Help!"

They all rushed over to help Marco and Petunia. All except Edmond, who stood apart, watching with his head tilted slightly to the side.

Holly gripped the bookcase and heaved with everything she had. The wood was thick and sturdy, but she could feel it beginning to scrape forward.

"A . . . little . . . more," Petunia said through clenched teeth.

Finally, Holly felt the weight of the bookcase shift, its top tilting away from the door. For a moment it stood perfectly on edge, then it tipped forward, crashing to the ground. It landed with a crack.

"Go!" Holly panted. "Let's go!"

Edmond was first to the door. He pulled it, but it only opened a small bit before it stopped, slamming into something solid and wooden. The bottom of the fallen bookcase was right in front of the door, still blocking it. There was only a narrow opening, just big enough for them to squeeze through one at a time.

Edmond quickly slipped through without a look back. Before anyone else could move, though, there was a loud, hollow thump from behind.

The witch had entered the room.

She held one hand against the wall, leaning against it. She seemed to still be weak, not fully recovered, but she strode forward anyway. She outstretched an arm, fingers opening and closing, grasping. She was right there, right in front of them, and there was no way they could all make it through the door fast enough.

Marco turned to Holly and Hector.

"Protect each other," he said to them.

"What?" Holly asked.

Marco gazed at her with wide, gentle, almost apologetic eyes.

He looks so much like Mom, she realized.

"And . . . remember us this time." He gave Holly a tiny, almost imperceptible wink. "OK?"

Then Marco ran toward *It*. He leapt on top of her, knocking her down.

"GO!" he screamed. "G—"

And his last words were swallowed as his body faded into stone.

21

"MARCO!" PETUNIA SCREAMED.

"Come on." George pulled at Holly and Hector, who were too shocked to move. "Don't let it be for nothing."

Behind them, the witch shivered and moaned. She was still on the ground, next to the statue of Marco. George pushed Hector through the narrow gap in the door, then quickly followed.

"We have to leave him." Petunia's eyes welled with tears. She took Holly's hand and led her outside to join the others.

There was a small drop from the door to the grass outside, and Holly almost tripped as she stumbled out. As soon as she and Petunia were outside, George slammed the door shut.

It was still night. The rain had cleared, and the sky was illuminated by a sea of stars and a bright, full moon. They were in a small, fenced-in area behind the church. The ground was overgrown with tall grass. It grew wild among small stone markers.

A graveyard.

Edmond faced them. His demeanor was unnaturally calm, as if nothing out of the ordinary had just happened.

"She will likely be out shortly," he said. He raised his eyebrows. There was a hint of a smile at the corner of his lips. "We should hide."

Something knocked against the back door of the church. There was scratching, like nails clawing on wood.

"That's her," Petunia whispered, her voice quivering.

"This way," Edmond said. He walked into the grave-yard. A tiny giggle escaped his mouth. "I have a secret. Hector knows."

Holly gave Hector a what-the-heck-does-that-mean look.

"It's OK," Hector said. "I think I know what he's talking about."

They followed Edmond. He bent his head low as he walked among the gravestones, all of them cluttered in un-even rows. The names and dates on the stones had been weathered and worn down by time, but some Holly could still make out. A first name: *Constance*. A date of birth: *1699*.

There was a loud, throaty grunt behind them, and then the *thump, thump* of something heavy moving behind the back door.

"Here we are." Edmond squatted next to a gravestone.

There was a name on it. *Thaddeus Vallens.* And a date. *1702–1739.* The ground in front of the marker was covered in leaves and twigs.

Edmond reached down and pulled the mass of branches up all at once. Holly saw now that they were bundled together, and beneath was a wide, dark hole.

It looked just like a grave.

Edmond slid into the hole and crouched down, disappearing.

"He wants us to hide in *there?*" Petunia gulped. "In someone's *grave?*"

Before Holly could respond, a chilling howl filled the air. Holly looked, and it was just as she feared. *It* was out of the church. She was in her wolf form, her eyes casting a red glow.

Quickly, they all tumbled into the hole together. The space wasn't big enough for all of them, and they wedged inside over and on top of one another, a mass of sweaty and tangled limbs. At last, Edmond managed to reach his hand up and pull the bundled branches back over their heads.

The air was warm and suffocating. Bodies pressed against Holly, forcing her to shift and squirm. She lost her balance, falling on someone else's back. She reached down to steady herself, and her hand closed against something smooth and solid.

A bone.

Had she just touched somebody's skull? Had she just

wrapped her hand around the remains of *Thaddeus Vallens*? Holly swallowed her urge to scream.

There were sounds from above. Paws on the grass. A searching, steady growl.

She's right above us. Holly felt sweat dripping down her cheek. She could hear someone—Hector? George?— taking shallow, ragged breaths. *If I can hear them, so can she,* Holly thought, but she didn't dare warn them. She couldn't speak; she could only crouch in the dark and the dirt, hoping *It* didn't find them, praying that she hadn't crawled into her own grave.

Claws scratched overhead. A single twig fell, landing on Holly's back.

Then something else. A soft sound, close by. Someone was whistling. It was a slow, sad song, each note sustained so long it seemed to be yearning for release, desperate for whatever came next.

Who could that be? Holly wondered.

Then came the sound of feathers rustling, of wings beating the air. Of a raven calling into the night.

Edmond stood and threw off the canopy of leaves.

"Ha!" he said, peering up at the sky. He looked pleased.

Holly disentangled herself from the others, and they all pushed and shoved as they hurried to climb out.

"Worst. Hiding. Spot. Ever," Petunia grunted.

They gathered around the tombstone, dusting them-selves off, and Edmond placed the cover over the hole once more. Petunia and Hector were looking around nervously, but George had his eyes locked on the church.

"We should go back," George said.

"Wait, what?" Holly blurted out. "That's crazy."

"No, it's *safe*," George said. "We survived for *months* in that church!" He then took his glasses off and covered his eyes. "Oh god . . . *we*. Javier. I can't believe . . ."

Petunia went to him and gently put a hand on his shoulder. "I'm sorry." She gave Holly a soft look. "We know what you're going through."

Now it was Holly's turn to stare sadly back at the church. Marco was in there. She had lost him, and only just after learning who he really was. There was so much she had wanted to ask him. She couldn't get his last words out of her mind. *Remember us this time.* She felt an emptiness in her gut, like something precious and vital had been stolen from her.

No, not just from her. From Hector too.

Hector approached Holly, looking worried. "Are you OK?"

How was she supposed to explain this to him? How could she tell him they had brothers they didn't even remember? And now they were gone.

"No," she answered. "I'm not. I just know I don't want to stay here anymore."

George brushed Petunia's hand off his shoulder. "Where should we go, then? Where else is safe?"

"I don't know!" Holly threw her arms up. "I mean, this is Covenant, right? There has to be more than just a church around here."

"Of course there is," Edmond said. *"Much* more."

Everyone turned to look at him.

"What do you mean?" Holly asked.

"The town is that way," Edmond said, pointing through the forest. He smiled. "Do you want to go?"

22

IT WAS FINALLY MORNING. HOLLY STOOD ON A GRASSY HILL, watching dawn break over the horizon. The hill overlooked a small village. Edmond had told the truth. There was much more here than just the church.

"Covenant," Holly said.

It was surreal to see this colonial version of her hometown. A large lawn, which must have been something like a village green or common area, lay at the center. Two cobblestone thoroughfares ran parallel to each other on either side of the green. Sturdy-looking brick buildings lined the roads—picturesque shops or homes, Holly guessed, most with dormer windows peeking from slanted roofs. Beyond, the outskirts were all fields and pastures, overgrown with tufts of weeds and wild grass. The river—the same one that had been so violent during the storm—ran behind the village, curling in a great arc back into the woods.

Beside her, Hector tried and failed to stifle a yawn. It

was contagious, and soon Holly and the rest of the group took turns covering their mouths.

It had been a tense, tiring trek from the church through the woods. Their progress had been slow. Before heading off, George led them to the nearby apple orchard he had mentioned earlier. Everyone besides Edmond ate, Hector chomping greedily through three apples, and they each carried one or two with them for later.

After eating, they followed Edmond into the woods. It had still been dark, but it didn't seem to affect Edmond's sense of direction at all, much to George's surprise.

George had actually been difficult, at first, wanting to know who this Edmond kid was, and how he knew so much. Petunia quickly whispered into George's ear, and whatever she said seemed to mollify him, though he still looked skeptical.

They trod carefully over brush and around trees, everyone mindful of staying quiet. Holly had insisted that Hector hold her hand the entire way. He objected, but she wasn't going to lose him again.

She still had to tell him about Marco and Max. She also wanted to know what he had been doing with Edmond and how much he had learned about the mysterious gray-haired boy. But she couldn't ask in front of Edmond, who never strayed too far from Hector's side.

"Look at the architecture," George said, pulling Holly out of her thoughts. "It's colonial."

Holly smiled at George, agreeing with him. Warmth and light were spreading over the village. Except, Holly noticed, for one spot at the far end of the village green. That space was occupied by a large cloud of fog. It was wide and thick, like an enormous, vaporous wall blocking off the back end of town.

Edmond had his gray eyes fixed on that spot.

"What is it?" Holly asked him.

"I . . . dislike the fog," he answered.

Holly nodded, as if that explained everything. They had been up all night, and she was too tired to think about anything but sleep. She wasn't alone. Petunia's posture was hunched, and she was rubbing her eyes. George kept stumbling in place, like standing was too much of an effort. Hector stared off into space, his eyes slowly closing, then popping open again every few seconds.

"We should find somewhere in town to rest," Holly said. "At least for a little while."

Everyone agreed, and they trekked down the hill and into the village. They first came to a one-story storefront made of brick. Its windows were caked with dirt, just like the windows of the church. A network of cobwebs clung to the corners of the windowsills. A sign hung out front: COBBLER.

George peered through one of the windows. "It's all so . . . old. Like, from hundreds of years ago."

"You think we went back in time?" Petunia asked.

"Not exactly," George said. "I think this is, like, a pocket dimension or something."

"Huh?" Petunia put her hands on her hips.

"Like, if someone put our town, Covenant, in a bubble, way back in the 1700s. And then there were two Covenants. One that went on, like normal. That's the one that we come from. But there's also this one, which has stayed the same for, like, three hundred years."

George's explanation was met with silence.

"I read a lot of comics." He shrugged.

"Edmond?" Holly turned to him. "You've been here the longest, right? What do you think?"

Edmond frowned, as if confused. "This is the Hiddenseek."

Petunia joined Holly next to Edmond. "Do you know where we should go next? Are we close to the way home?"

A look of annoyance passed over Edmond's face at the mention of *home*, but it quickly vanished as he peered at the mass of fog at the far end of town. "We should . . . wait."

Hector went to the door of the cobbler shop. He tried the handle, but it didn't open. "Locked."

"Wait," Holly said. "George, remember the letter in the Bible? From Abigail?"

"Uh, *yeah*," he said. "I'm the one who found it."

"The millinery shop. We should look for that."

"Of course!" George snapped his fingers.

"What's a millinery shop?" Hector asked.

"Well, the more modern definition would be hat store," George answered. "Buuuuuut—"

"But colonial milliners sold more than just hats," Holly chimed in.

George smiled at her and held out his hand for a fist bump. "Team Paying Attention on Field Trips."

Hector rolled his eyes.

They found the shop that said MILLINERY out front only two buildings down. Holly checked, and sure enough, it was next to the forge, just like the letter from Abigail had said. Luckily, this time the front door was unlocked, and they all shuffled inside.

The shop walls were lined with hats and bonnets adorned with ribbons and ruffled lace. There were also patterned dresses on display, each outfitted with lace-trimmed petticoats, aprons, frilly neckerchiefs—all the accoutrements that filled out a colonial-era wardrobe. Everything was spotted and browned with age and had a thick patina of dust over it.

"Huh." Petunia sniffed. There was definitely an odor about the place, the mustiness of cloth slowly decaying over centuries.

Hector dropped to the floor, lying down on his back, his arms spread wide. George quickly followed him.

Holly wanted to explore, to search for anything that might have been left behind by Abigail, but she was so tired. She lay down on the floor. It wasn't exactly comfortable, but they had a roof over their heads, and nothing was chasing them. For the moment, at least, Holly let herself relax.

"Wait," Petunia said. She dashed to the shelves, returning with an armload of uncut fabric. She tossed it down. "Blankets." She smiled. "Or close enough."

"Good idea," George said, grabbing one from the stack.

They each took a blanket, wrapping themselves and getting comfortable. Except for Edmond, who folded his blanket neatly and sat on it, his legs crossed and his posture perfectly straight.

"Man." Petunia stretched. "I haven't slept with a blanket since I don't know when." She chuckled. "Well, since Oliver showed up and dragged me off. That's what I get for showing off, I guess. I just *knew* I could hide somewhere my cousins would never find me. And guess what? They never did! Just gave up looking." She made a *tsk* sound with her tongue as they all settled in. "What about you, George? How'd it happen for you?"

George adjusted his glasses, his face turning red. That seemed to happen a lot. "My birthday party. Went under my bed to hide and, um . . . fell asleep."

"What?" Petunia laughed.

"I was tired." George shrugged. "I had a lot of cake."

Petunia laughed some more, but Holly couldn't join in. She knew what was coming next. They were going to ask her how she had gotten here. She looked at Hector. He wasn't smiling either.

"Edmond," Holly said, hoping to delay the inevitable for as long as possible. "How did you first come to the Hiddenseek?"

"I think . . ." Edmond said, his gray eyes growing distant, "I think I've always been here. I don't like talking about it. It's not very fun."

Hearing the word *fun* caused Petunia to sit straight up. Holly remembered. *That's why he left Marco, Max, and Petunia. He said he wasn't having any fun.*

"Don't worry about it, Edmond," Petunia said, glaring at him. "You don't have to say *anything*. What about you two?" She pointed to Hector and Holly. "You came here together, right? How did that work?"

Hector frowned at Holly. He was shaking his head no.

Seeing that made Holly instantly angry. He was still just thinking about himself. Why *shouldn't* she tell everyone what had happened?

"Hector and his friends tricked me into playing hide-and-seek," she said. "Then they left me in the park."

"Holly!" Hector yelled.

"What? It's the truth."

Holly had missed Hector so much when they'd been separated. She'd been scared that he'd be lost forever. But that didn't mean she didn't deserve to be mad. *Of course* she was still mad.

Hector kicked his blanket off. "It's not that simple."

"Sure it is," Holly said. "I'm here, and it's your fault. See? Simple."

"I'm here *too*," he whined.

"Also your fault."

"Ugh." Hector stood. He grabbed his blanket and stomped over to the far end of the store. He curled up in a corner, his back to everyone.

"Hector," Petunia called to him.

"Let him sulk," Holly huffed.

"Come on. He's your brother."

"Whatever." Holly rolled her eyes. "If we're going to rest, let's rest."

Edmond got up and walked to the back of shop, near Hector. He didn't say anything. He sat down with his back to Hector, facing Holly and the others. It was almost like he was standing guard.

Petunia and George gave each other a look, but eventually put their heads down.

Soon all was silent.

Holly closed her eyes. She didn't know why Hector was so upset. He knew what he had done. If he didn't like her talking about it, he shouldn't have done it in the first place.

Finally, exhaustion took over. As Holly drifted off to sleep, though, Petunia's words rang in her ears: *He's your brother.*

Yeah. He was her brother.

That was why it still hurt.

23

A COLD TOUCH ON THE ARM NUDGED HECTOR AWAKE.

"Huh?" he said. "Holly?"

He opened his eyes. It wasn't Holly.

Edmond stood over him, holding a finger to his lips. He pointed to the door, then motioned for Hector to come with him.

Hector got up and followed. They snuck past Petunia and George, who were still sprawled out on the floor, clutching their makeshift blankets. He didn't see Holly, though. He tried not to worry. *Probably went to the bathroom somewhere,* he told himself. She wouldn't just leave him, no matter how angry she was.

Edmond gently pushed the front door open, and he and Hector slipped through.

"Keep your voice low," Edmond said. "I wouldn't want to wake the others."

Hector squinted. The sun was now high in the sky. "OK. What is it? Is it Holly?"

"In a sense." Edmond gave a small, formal bow. "Are you ready to depart?"

"Huh?"

"We found your sister," Edmond said. "Now we can play a new game."

At first Hector thought he was joking, but his face was completely serious.

"Edmond," Hector said. "I don't know what you're talking about. We're not *playing* anything. We're trying to get home."

"I *knew* you would say that." Edmond harrumphed. "Why does everyone only want to go home?"

"Why?" Hector sputtered. "So we don't end up as statues? So we can see our families again?" He sighed. "So Holly doesn't hate me anymore."

"Your sister." Edmond scowled. "You are quarreling with her."

"Ha. Yeah. Quarreling." Hector laughed. Edmond had such a strange way of talking. "She just *had* to make sure everyone knows what a screwup I am. No big deal."

"She *upset* you," Edmond said.

"She always thinks she's better than me. At *everything*. Just once I'd like to . . ." Hector trailed off. Something had occurred to him. "Hey, you know the way home, right? That's what you said, back when we first met."

Edmond just stared at Hector. It was weird.

"Do you think you could tell me?" Hector asked. If Hector figured out the way home, that would *totally* make up for everything. He'd be the hero. Holly would forgive him for sure.

"If I tell you," Edmond said, "you'll leave."

"Um, yes," Hector said. "That would be the point."

A cloud seemed to pass over Edmond's face. He glowered, his gray, unblinking eyes boiling with mounting fury.

Then, suddenly, his expression cleared. A look of understanding dawned on Edmond. He began bobbing his head up and down, as if agreeing to something. Slowly, he gave Hector a tight, closed-lipped smile.

"I'm going to help you," he said. "I'm going to tell you exactly what to do."

24

18th August, 1737
Dear Abigail,

    I expect this letter to find you in a more composed and agreeable humor than when last we met. Coming to the manor uninvited was, on its own, a breach of etiquette. Your belligerent disposition toward my wife was unacceptable; your accusations of witchcraft unfounded; and your loss of control an embarrassment for all involved.

    I have negotiated an extension of your lodgings at the millinery shop. This arrangement will expire in three months' time. Following that, your fate is your own.

    You will find enclosed a small sum of money, which I expect you to squander, but which I hope you will prudently apply toward securing a more stable position *within the community. I have also sent a tincture adequate for calming your nerves, prepared by my wife. There is no witchcraft in it. The ingredients are all of nature, including a modicum of generosity and goodwill, qualities in which I find you to be harmfully deficient. I hardly recognize in you now the joyful companion that you were to me in our youth.*

These shall be my final words on this matter, and to you.

Your brother no more,
Oliver

Holly came to the end of the letter. She lingered on the last line for a moment. Was that really possible? she wondered. Had he really done that, cut his sister out of his life forever? Then her eyes jumped back to the top, reading the entire letter again.

She had woken before the others, too anxious to begin searching the shop for anything that Abigail might have left behind. She had tiptoed around them and found a narrow wooden staircase leading to a small apartment on the second floor.

The room was cluttered with fabric and sewing materials, including an old-fashioned spinning wheel that still held a large spool of thread. There was also a little cot in the back, and underneath it, Holly had found a stack of letters.

Most were mundane or didn't reveal anything new. There was a response from the pastor Abigail had written to, but he mostly just quoted from Scripture.

This letter, though, was the clue she had been looking for. The manor. The home of the witch. Holly bet there would be even more clues there, maybe even the way back home, if that was where the witch actually lived.

And then there was the small matter of how the letter was signed.

Your brother no more, Oliver.

What were the odds that this was a different Oliver? An Oliver who just happened to be married to someone who might be a witch? A witch who could turn into a raven?

Oliver was married to the woman in black. Oliver was married to *It.*

Holly heard voices downstairs. Everyone else was finally awake. She couldn't wait to tell them what she'd found. She grasped the letter and bounded down the stairs.

"But why would Edmond just tell you?" George was asking Hector. "Why not take us there himself?"

"He doesn't really like the rest of you," Hector said. "Sorry."

Petunia scowled. "I *knew* this would happen."

Holly joined them. "What's going on?"

Petunia folded her arms and glared at Hector. "Edmond left."

"He left?" Holly said. "Why? Where did he go?"

Hector spun around, triumphant. He was beaming with pride. "Edmond told me where to go! He told me the way *home!*"

"Let me guess," Holly said. "It's at a manor house."

George's and Petunia's mouths popped open with surprise. Hector rolled his eyes and muttered something under his breath.

"How did you know that?" George asked.

Holly unfolded the letter from Oliver. "I found this upstairs. Take a look."

George took the letter and read it out loud. He and Petunia had the same shocked reaction as Holly.

"Oliver is married to *It*?" Petunia said. "Ewww!"

"This confirms that they lived in a manor," George said. "That's Hector's story too."

"It's not a *story,*" Hector said defensively. "It's true. Edmond *told* me. Plus, he said the exit is in a fountain. You didn't find *that* in a letter."

"Wait, what do you mean by *exit*?" George asked.

"I mean the way *home!*" Hector said, sounding exasperated.

Holly narrowed her eyes at Hector. "Did he say what we should do at the fountain?"

"No." Hector frowned.

"Did he say where the fountain was?"

"No."

"Did you ask?"

"No."

"Why didn't you ask?"

"Because I *didn't*!" Hector yelled. "Sorry I didn't do everything *perfectly*!"

Everyone stared at Hector. His face quickly went from angry to embarrassed.

"Um, good work," George said, awkwardly breaking the silence. "Everyone. Real good work."

They decided to leave right away, to make the most of the daylight. There was no telling what they would encounter at this manor house, and they all agreed that it would be too risky to search it at night in the dark.

They finished off their apples for breakfast and exited the millinery shop onto the cobblestone thoroughfare. From the position of the sun, it looked to be sometime in the afternoon. The weather was cool, like that of early spring. But all was gray and dim. Even the sun seemed subdued, its light weak and dull, as if covered by a veil. They had stepped inside a shadow, Holly felt, and like a shadow, the veil of gloom clung to them, following them, never letting go.

The manor house, according to Hector, was at the end of the street, in front of the village green. But if there was a house there, it was obscured by the wall of fog Holly had noticed earlier. It loomed before them like a dark thundercloud, stretching across the village and into the fields and forest beyond.

Just at the edge of the foreboding mist, there was an oxcart, empty and abandoned.

"That's . . ." George pointed.

"Oliver," Holly said. "He must be near." She glanced around nervously. She had no idea what Oliver might be doing here, and she didn't want to find out. "We should hurry and find the house."

"I'm not going through that fog," Hector said. "Edmond was scared of it."

"We can look for a way around," George suggested.

Holly approached cautiously. The fog itself was mesmerizing. It swirled and shifted as if agitated. As if alive. There were dark shadows, too, deep inside. The shadows almost looked like people, their long arms waving, beckoning.

"Holly," George said. "Careful. Back up from there."

"OK," she said, but she didn't move. *What if there is no way around the fog?* she wondered. They'd have to go through it anyway. They'd just be wasting time, wasting daylight.

"Holly!" George shouted.

A wisp of fog lashed out like a tentacle, striking Holly, swirling around her. She felt it pulling her, reeling her in.

"Help!" Holly shouted.

George, Petunia, and Hector ran to her. They grabbed her, trying to yank her back. But the fog encircling Holly split apart. It spread, surrounding them. In moments it covered them completely.

133

Then all was cold and lost and endlessly dark.

"What did you do?" Hector shouted at her.

"Nothing!" Holly yelled back, but the fog whirled and howled around them, swallowing her words, swallowing everything.

At last the fog cleared, parting like a curtain drawn back at the opening of a play.

Holly realized they were indoors. Inside a house. In a hallway. There was a picture on the wall.

A picture she would have recognized anywhere.

25

HOLLY STARED AT THE PHOTO. THERE WAS HECTOR, SLIDING OFF
his seat. There was Holly, frowning. Mom and Dad with
their plastic smiles. And two boys, both with identical satisfied looks on their faces.

Marco and Max.

"What happened?" George spun around, as if trying to
make sense of his surroundings. "Where are we?"

"This is our house!" Hector tugged at Holly. He was
bursting with joy. "We're home!"

Petunia turned to Holly. "Is that true?" Her voice was
full of hope.

"Yes," Holly confirmed. "This is definitely our house."

Petunia made a noise that was something between a
gasp and a laugh. "We made it," she whispered. "We actually made it."

George, Petunia, and Hector began to celebrate,

sharing exuberant smiles and hugs. But Holly held back from the others. Something was off. The hallway seemed like it was just slightly the wrong color. Everything was dull and muted, like an old photograph aged by time. It made her feel uneasy.

A door opened, and someone stepped out into the hall. A girl. She had a long black braid. Just like her mother's.

It was Holly. She was looking at herself.

Holly stepped out of the way, making room for this other version of herself to walk past. Her doppelganger didn't see or acknowledge her presence in any way.

"Holly?" Petunia asked. The smile on her face was fading. "Is that . . . you?"

The other Holly didn't so much walk as stomp down the hall. It was an almost perfect imitation of her mom when she was angry.

"She didn't see us," George said. "It's like we weren't even there."

"This is weird," Hector said. "What's going on?"

"I don't know," Holly answered. She heard voices coming from the front of the house. "But I want to find out."

They filed down the hall and into the living room. The other Holly was standing right in front of the TV, blocking it. She was shaking her finger at two boys sitting in front of her. Marco and Max.

The twins were sprawled out on the floor, each with a

136

video-game controller in hand. They looked as relaxed and comfortable as possible. They looked at home.

"You're not hiding," the other Holly said.

"C'mon." Marco leaned to look past Holly. "Move out of the way!"

Hector took a step forward as if to get a better look. "What are those guys doing here?" he asked, sounding utterly confused.

"Is that . . . ?" Petunia squinted, then she whipped around to face Holly. When she spoke, her voice shook. "Holly? What is this? Why are Marco and Max in your house?"

Holly could see the pain on Petunia's face. She could hear it in her voice. *She thinks we lied to her, that we hid it from her.*

"I'm sorry," Holly said. "It's not what it looks like. I was going to tell you." She turned to Hector. "Tell you both."

"Tell me what?" Hector asked.

"They're our brothers," Holly said.

"Brothers?" Hector scoffed. "We don't have brothers." A look of doubt crossed his face, though.

Before Holly could respond, another version of Hector walked in from the hallway. The real Hector's mouth dropped open.

"Why aren't we playing yet?" the other Hector asked.

"They're not hiding." The other Holly scrunched her face up in anger.

Holly felt a rush of embarrassment. *Do I really look like that?*

Petunia grabbed Holly by the shoulder to turn her back around. "Why didn't you say anything?"

"I didn't know, not at first," Holly explained.

"What do you mean? How could you not know?" Petunia was incredulous.

"Wait," George said, stepping between them. "Remember what Oliver told us? That no one would re-member us?"

Petunia began to retort, then stopped, swallowing her words. A lightbulb seemed to have clicked in her head. "Oliver took them first," she said to Holly. "You forgot them."

Holly gave Petunia a sad nod.

"I think . . . maybe I saw their room . . ." Hector looked back toward the hall.

The extra room in the hallway. The door Holly had never opened. *Of course.* It belonged to the twins.

Holly quickly scanned the living room, looking for other small differences. She noticed now that things seemed more organized, tidier. The way it looked before Mom had changed.

"I think we're somehow in the past," Holly said. "Like in a memory that we lost."

"Holly! Heads up!"

They all jumped at the other Hector's sudden shout. He tossed something to the other Holly. She caught it.

"Look what I've got," she teased. "Max's phone."

"Whatever," Max said, still intent on his game. "You don't know the passcode."

"Let's see," the other Holly said. "With Max, it would be something needlessly complicated but still uncreative—"

"Ouch." Marco laughed.

"Your birthday." The other Holly started thumbing the phone. "But the numbers rearranged in a sequential order . . . There. Huh. How 'bout that? First try."

Holly cringed. This other version of herself sounded so . . . arrogant.

Max dropped his controller and hopped up. "Hey! Give it back!"

"Hide-and-seek." The other Holly was emphatic.

"Ugh." Max rubbed his hands over his eyes. "Whose idea was babysitting?"

"Yours," Marco said.

"I'm an idiot. Fine. We'll play."

Petunia covered her mouth. She looked stricken. "Hide-and-seek. They're playing hide-and-seek."

The other Hector began counting.

The other Holly pulled at Marco's shirt. "Let's all hide outside," she whispered in his ear. "Hector won't look for us there."

The twins agreed, and they all quietly snuck out the back. A few seconds later, the other Holly ran back inside. She clicked the lock in place.

She had locked Marco and Max out of the house.

The other Hector had a video-game controller in his hand. "Victory! The game is ours!" The other Holly sat down with him to play.

"Oh no." Holly's stomach sank. She could practically hear Oliver's voice in her head. *You hid. But you were not found.* She watched the other Holly laughing and gloating. She looked so pleased with herself.

"How could you?" Petunia's eyes were red. Her face swelled with anger. "They were *good*," she practically spat. "They helped me. They helped *you!*"

"I'm sorry," Holly said.

She felt guilty. Even though she had no memory of what she had done, she had still done it. She had sent Marco and Max to the Hiddenseek.

A gust of wind whipped through Holly's hair. This made no sense. They were indoors, but now there was a chill and a breeze. Then she saw the mist. It seeped in from under the front door, through the cracks in the walls. It poured from the vents.

The fog gathered. They all bunched together as if in the eye of a hurricane, gray clouds swirling around them. The house, the other versions of Holly and Hector, everything but the fog was gone.

The wind picked up. There was a whistling sound, like air escaping a balloon. A small hole appeared in the fog. It expanded. It looked like a large circular window, through which Holly could see sunlight and perhaps even a hint of green grass or trees.

It looked like a way out.

"Follow me!" Holly shouted, trying to raise her voice over the rushing wind. George shouted something back, but she couldn't hear.

The hole began to shrink. It was closing.

Holly locked arms with Hector and pulled him with her. George and Petunia followed. They ran toward the hole, pressing forward against the wind. The exit continued to shrink, the fog closing in like water circling a drain.

Holly sprinted with all she had. She reached out just in time to see the hole disappear, tufts of mist wafting over her outstretched hand.

She was too late.

26

WHEN AT LAST THE FOG BEGAN TO CLEAR, WHEN THE BLURRY, blinding gray finally calmed and broke apart, the first thing Holly saw was grass. It was a narrow patch of lawn, just next to a curb. She was on a sidewalk.

"Where are we now?" Hector spun around, searching. The fog was dissipating slowly, and it was still difficult to see.

"I can't tell," George said. "Looks like we're outdoors."

Petunia sank to the ground, burying her face in her hands. "I'm so tired of this stupid place," she cried in muffled sobs. "I just want to go home."

"Hey." Holly reached out to comfort her, but Petunia wouldn't even look at her.

"Don't talk to me." She waved Holly away.

Holly drew back. *She blames me for the twins,* Holly thought. She wished she could think of something to say to make it better. She wished she didn't feel like it really was all her fault.

The sound of chattering and laughter came from behind.

"Ha ha! Did you see her face?"

Holly turned toward the voices. She had been so preoccupied, she hadn't even noticed that the fog had fully cleared.

They were just outside a park. There was a playground. A very familiar playground.

This was *her* park. This was where she had been hiding when all of this began.

A group of kids came down the sidewalk. She recognized them. Owen Orlofsky, Karen Graham, Zoe Zamarripa.

And Hector. Well, the past version of Hector.

They were all smiling and laughing.

"Did you see the way she ran?" Zoe sneered. "I'm embarrassed for her. I really am."

Correction, Holly thought. They were all smiling and laughing *at her.*

"She thinks she's so smart." The other Hector eyed the playground, where the other Holly was hiding.

The snickering kids walked off together, away from the park. Hector stopped to look back, once, before he left her behind.

Holly had known how they must have laughed at her.

She'd imagined what they must have said. But seeing it, actually seeing Hector join in, was so much worse. Her entire body felt wounded and raw.

This is what he really thinks of me. What they all really think.

"Holly." The real Hector's quiet voice came from beside her. "I didn't mean it."

As if she could believe that. As if it even mattered now.

"Just shut up," Holly said.

The memory kept playing, right in front of their eyes. The other Hector came back. He skulked around the corner, hiding behind a bench. Holly didn't know he'd done that. She could see his face. He was smiling.

Holly watched the past version of herself crawl out from her hiding spot in the tunnel. Tears streaked her face. She could sense George and Petunia staring at her, pitying her. She couldn't meet their eyes.

Fog rolled in, just as it had before. It settled over the park, slowly stretching, expanding. *It's coming for us,* Holly realized. It quickly surrounded them again.

"Holly, listen—" Hector started.

"Not *now*, dummy!" Holly snapped. "Didn't I say to shut up?"

"No!" Hector shouted back, his voice cracking. "I WON'T shut up!"

A whistling sound filled the air. Behind Hector, right

by the tunnel where Holly had hidden, a small hole in the fog appeared. The exit.

"And I'm NOT a dummy!" Hector kept shouting. "I *hate* when you call me that." His cheeks were getting red, and he had that expression on his face. Mouth open, bottom teeth starting to stick out. A meltdown.

He can't seriously be doing this right now.

"We don't have time for this!" Holly yelled. "We have to go! Now!"

"NO!" Hector cried. "I'm not going ANYWHERE with you!"

The hole in the fog had expanded. It was big enough to run through, but if this was anything like the last time, in moments, it would be closed.

Holly grabbed her brother by the arm. She was going to save his stupid life. Then she was going to tell him *exactly* what she thought of him, once and for all.

27

THEY EMERGED FROM THE FOG, STUMBLING LIKE DAZED survivors coming ashore after a shipwreck. Holly still held on to Hector's arm. Behind her, Petunia and George tumbled to the ground. Everything was still blurry, but something ahead dominated her field of vision, something tall and solid.

The manor.

It was old. Not just in style, though that was old too. Its façade was rectangular and flat, made of once-red bricks that were now blotched with black and gray. A set of double doors—white paint peeling and cracking off in jagged strips—separated the two wings of the house. Each side was a mirror image of the other. There were two rows of windows, each one dark and cloudy like eyes that had gone blind.

George rested with his hands on his knees, catching

his breath. Petunia spun slowly around, as if unsure which direction to go.

Hector yanked his arm away from Holly's grasp, hard. She turned on him.

"What was that all about in there?" she demanded.

He rolled his eyes. "Forget it."

She wasn't going to let him off that easy this time. "You always do this. You only ever think about *yourself*. It's always all about *you*."

"And you always do *this*," Hector snapped. "You always think you know *everything*. You always act like you're *better* than me." His face was red and sizzling. *"I'm sick of it!"* He took sharp, angry breaths and glared at Holly. Like *she* was the one who had done something wrong.

Holly was incredulous. "Really?" Now she was even angrier. *"That's* why you left me in the park? *That's* why you got us into this mess?"

"No," Hector said. *"That's* why no one likes you. *That's* why you don't have any friends."

His words hung in the air. Holly didn't respond. Not right away. The silence was its own kind of response. It let him know this wasn't just an argument. Not anymore.

"You're right," Holly said.

That was not what Hector had expected to hear. He opened then closed his mouth, unsure of how to respond.

Holly's voice was just a scratch above a whisper. "I don't

have any friends." Hector's expression softened. Maybe it was a sign of regret. Holly didn't care. "And I don't have a brother now either. Once we get home, I'm done with you."

Hector's eyes twitched. A little. But he didn't break eye contact. Holly and Hector stared each other down, both defiant, both daring the other to look away first.

"Good," Hector said.

"Good," Holly replied.

"Guys." A voice from behind broke their standoff. It was Petunia. "Can we leave now?" She had her arms crossed, her eyes shooting daggers at them. "Can we try to go home?"

Petunia was right, of course. They were wasting time. Holly could hear Hector shuffling behind her, but she didn't turn or acknowledge him in any way. Best to ignore him.

"OK." Holly nodded. "Let's go."

The four of them slumped over to the house, dragging themselves across the lawn. No one spoke.

"Wait," George said as Holly reached for the handle. "Don't we need to get around to the back? That's where a fountain would be, right?"

"Yeah," Holly said. "But look." She pointed. Fog surrounded the sides of the house, curling and slapping against the walls as if trying to break its way in. "I'm not going back in that stuff. Not if I can help it."

George nodded his agreement. Holly twisted the

handle, and the door creaked open. They stepped inside.

A foyer spread before them in an oval. The walls were adorned in decorative mahogany paneling. There was a red tasseled rug in the center, covering a dark wooden floor. Beyond the foyer was a hallway, stretching back to a staircase.

And in the center of the foyer was a statue.

It was a child on his knees. A boy, wearing pants that came down only to his calves. The boy had his hands together. The plaintive expression forever etched on his face made it seem like he was begging. Or sending a prayer that was never answered.

His eyes flashed red.

"Close the door!" Holly yelled. George slammed the door shut. "We'll have time if we hurry," Holly told the others. "We just need to get through the house and out back."

As if in answer, there was a heavy, hollow thump. Then another. And another. The woman in black stood at the bottom of the stairs.

She was already there.

The woman spread her arms and leapt, her black dress and hair flowing and wrapping around her as she sprouted wings. She was the raven, streaking toward them like an unleashed arrow.

"This way!" Holly yelled, quickly running forward. If they got past her, maybe they could get outside to the

149

fountain before she caught up. Holly slid beneath the gliding raven.

But Hector, Petunia, and George hadn't moved fast enough.

It landed. Black feathers stretched and billowed and snapped just as she touched ground. She rose, once again the woman.

She was between Holly and the others.

George, Petunia, and Hector backed away, edging around the curve of the foyer. But *It* ignored them. She turned fully around to face Holly. Her red eyes sparked like flames.

Holly had no choice. She spun around. There was only one way to go. She raced for the stairs.

Whatever happened next, she would have to face it on her own.

28

HOLLY TOOK THE STAIRS TWO AT A TIME. SHE GOT TO A SHORT landing, where the stairs turned, grabbed the handrail, and swung herself around. As she pivoted, she saw *It* coming up behind her. The woman in black didn't rush. She climbed slowly, deliberately. She walked as if she had all the time in world.

These must be the only stairs, Holly thought. *She must know I'm trapped.*

Holly leapt over the final two steps and landed on the second floor. She was in a dimly lit and narrow hallway. The walls here were marred by deep scratches, like a wild animal had been set loose inside. *Like a wolf,* Holly realized.

Thump. Thump.

The sound of feet on the staircase spurred Holly forward. There were four doors in the hall to choose from. One on her left already stood open. She lunged inside.

It was a bedroom. A four-poster bed festooned in flower-print curtains lay at the center. Holly quickly scanned the rest of the room—there were a nightstand and vanity near the bed, and a bookcase against the far wall. There was also a window, and even through the layers of dust and filth, Holly could see movement. It was the fog, beating against the glass from the outside.

Holly dropped to her stomach and crawled under the bed, turning so that her eyes would face the door.

I should have closed that, Holly thought.

She watched as pale bare feet, poking out from beneath the tattered hem of a flowing black dress, stepped into the room, then stopped.

Holly held her breath. She didn't dare move. She fought to ignore her body's urge to run, to squirm, to shrink away.

The woman's feet moved again, a step closer.

Holly closed her eyes, as if blocking her sight was a sort of hiding. She wondered if this was where she would end up forever. A statue under a bed.

CLUNK!

A loud crash came from below. From downstairs. Holly popped her eyes open.

The feet turned away from the bed and back toward the door.

The woman slipped out of the room. Holly listened to the sounds of her footsteps moving away, getting faster.

She was gone.

She's going after the others, Holly thought.

Part of her wanted to stay under the bed. To never come out. But there was no time for that. She needed to get downstairs and help. She didn't know what she could do, but she had to try.

She got out from under the bed and took one step toward the door. And then the door moved. By itself. It swung, slowly closing.

But it had not, in fact, moved by itself.

Someone was hiding behind it.

First, Holly could see a pale hand, its fingers splayed against the door, pushing it. Then she could see bare feet protruding from worn, tattered trousers. Finally, she saw him, his gray eyes, his pale, grim complexion.

Edmond.

"Hello, Holly," he said. His voice was calm, but there was a hint of something else in it. Something that made Holly wary.

Questions ran through her head. *Where have you been? Is this really the way home? Can you help?* But she didn't ask them. The look on Edmond's face stopped her.

"You are good at playing," Edmond said. "Better than I expected."

"What do you mean, Edmond?" Holly tried to make her voice sound natural. "What are you talking about?"

"I thought he would be by himself by now. That would have been so much easier." Edmond came closer to Holly.

He had one hand behind his back. She instinctively leaned away.

"Edmond, please," Holly said. She didn't even know what she was asking him to do. She just knew that whatever he had planned wasn't good.

He took his hand from behind his back. He was holding something metal, something pointy. Holly jumped.

It was a key.

"You'll be safe here," Edmond said. "We'll take care of you."

"We? We who?" Holly asked. But she already knew.

"Hector and me," Edmond said. "He is going to be just like me. Soon. We'll have so much fun together."

Just like him? What did Edmond mean?

"No," Holly pleaded. "Please, we just want to go home. Don't you want to go home?"

Edmond smiled. "I am home."

He backed away from her. He reached behind him, grasping the doorknob.

"Wait!" Holly ran forward. She had to stop him. She couldn't let him leave the room.

But she wasn't quick enough.

Edmond slammed the door right in her face. She grabbed the doorknob and twisted just as she heard a small, metallic click. The door rattled in place, but it didn't open.

Holly was locked inside.

29

"WHAT ABOUT HOLLY?" HECTOR SAID.

After *It* appeared, George and Petunia had dragged Hector into another room, slamming the door shut behind them. The last thing he had seen was the woman in black climbing the stairs, going after Holly.

They were in what appeared to be some sort of study or parlor. The center of the room was set up for conversation, with a dingy blue couch and a couple of straight-backed, uncomfortable-looking chairs. A rickety gateleg side table held some little porcelain teacups, their insides moldy and gross. Somber-faced painted portraits with ornamental gold frames hung on the walls.

"I don't know." George started pacing around in a small circle. "I don't know what to do."

Hector reached for the door. "We need to go help her."

"No!" George grabbed Hector's hand. "You'll just get *us* caught too!"

"What do you mean *too*?" Hector snatched his hand away. "She's not caught yet." She couldn't be.

George knelt down into a little ball, covering his head. "We have to get out, we have to get out . . ." he kept repeating.

Petunia had wandered over to the portraits. She was staring up at them, mesmerized, like she was at a museum.

George sprang up. "The windows!"

There were a couple of windows on the back wall, their glass panels smudged up like every other window in this place. George started fumbling around at the windowsill.

"Guys," Hector said. "*Please*. We need to do something to help Holly."

"Have you seen these?" Petunia said, still looking up at the portraits. "They look familiar . . ."

Hector took a second to glance. They didn't seem all that remarkable. There were four portraits on the wall. One was of a man, looking stern, wearing one of those old-timey wigs with the long curls. Another was of a woman in a white dress with long black hair. And then there were two children, one blond, the other with brown hair.

The blond-haired kid caught Hector's eye. The way his head was slightly tilted. The serious expression. Hector *did* recognize him.

It was Edmond.

"They're stuck!" yelled George desperately.

He picked up a small table and tossed it at the window.

It landed with a crash, bursting apart. Wood splintered and scattered across the floor.

The window hadn't even cracked.

"What are you *doing*?" Hector asked.

"I don't know." George looked completely lost. "I don't know."

THUMP THUMP THUMP THUMP.

Someone was coming down the stairs. Fast.

"Hide," George said.

There weren't many places to choose from. Hector and George both went to the other side of the couch and squatted behind it. Petunia, though, remained in the middle of the room.

"Petunia!" George hissed at her. "Hide!"

The door opened. Hector, tucked behind the couch, couldn't see who had entered. But he could hear footsteps. Bare feet on wood.

Petunia turned at the sound. Her mouth dropped open, and her eyes went wide with fear.

"No," she said. She backed away, but there was nowhere to go except up against the wall.

More footsteps, now on carpet.

"Help," Petunia said. "Someone help."

George closed his eyes tight. He began muttering something under his breath.

The woman in black came into view. Her back was to Hector.

If she's here, maybe Holly got away, he thought. *Or maybe she got caught.*

It stepped right in front of Petunia. Her hand was out, ready to grab the girl, to turn her to stone.

"Please," Petunia whimpered. All hope had drained from her voice.

"I can't, I can't, I can't . . ." George repeated. Then he stood. "I can't just do nothing. Not again."

George screamed at the top of his lungs. It was a roar, a battle cry. It was everything George had bottled up inside coming out all at once, for all to hear.

It turned to face him.

George charged. He slammed into *It* like a linebacker, wrapping his arms around her waist, driving her to the ground. They both crashed to the floor, George on top.

"Run, Petunia!" he yelled.

Petunia didn't hesitate. She sprinted from her spot against the wall and out the door.

It rolled over, pinning George underneath her. He kicked his legs, squirming. He swiped at her arms, trying to hold her back. But she swatted his hands away with a single, swift motion, like a scythe cutting through wheat. She raised her arm as if in triumph, then brought it down, slamming her palm over his face.

"Go!" George gasped with his last breath, slapping her hand off his face. Then he went still. The color drained from his body, and he became stone, caught forever in his last act, fighting and defiant.

It tumbled off George and onto the floor. She moaned, grabbing her stomach and curling up in pain.

Hector had to get out of the room as quickly as possible. George had given him a chance to escape, to run upstairs and find Holly. He quietly edged against a bookcase along the wall, making his way toward the door.

Behind him, the wall moved.

Hector jumped. The bookcase swung open. It was a door. A secret passage.

Edmond emerged from the passageway. "Hector, you must hurry. Come with me."

"No," Hector said. "Holly . . ." With all that had just happened, that was as much as he could get out.

"I know where she is," Edmond said. "Quickly. She needs our help." Edmond reached out, inviting Hector to take his hand.

Hector took it.

30

HOLLY HEARD THE COMMOTION DOWNSTAIRS—RUNNING, yelling, the sound of someone or something falling.

And then there was silence.

She pulled on the door handle, trying in vain to open it. *Stupid.* She knew it wasn't going to work. She would have to think of something else. She needed to get out of this room. There was no telling what was happening to the others. Or what Edmond planned to do with Hector.

She looked around the bedroom, searching for something, anything that might help her escape. There was only the four-poster bed, the bookcase, the nightstand, and the vanity.

And the window.

Holly went to it. She could see the faint movement of the fog outside. She put a hand on the window, but left it there. She wouldn't open it. Not yet. She'd only risk it as a last resort.

Maybe there's another key, she thought.

She moved to the nightstand. Resting on top were a washbasin and a pitcher. Both looked heavy and solid. The stand also had a drawer. Holly pulled it open.

There wasn't much inside. A silver ring. A necklace. And an envelope, sealed on the back with a mound of wax.

Holly took the envelope out of the drawer. There was a name written on the front.

Oliver.

She ran a finger along the seal, briefly hesitating. Then she peeled the wax off, tossing it on the ground. She opened the envelope, revealing a two-page letter inside. The handwriting was flowing and elegant, each word closing with a swooping flourish.

17th December, 1737

My dearest husband,

You will never read these words. They are for my benefit alone. My small way of salving grief. By the time the ink is dry, you may have already passed into the next life.

All my arts have failed. I could not save you. Not with the tinctures I fed you while you were still conscious. Not with the secret ministrations I applied while you slept. All have broken at the wall of your illness.

I was never as facile with healing as I was with the

more destructive aspects of the arts. I fear what that reveals about me. I confess the satisfaction I felt when you delivered my potion, unaware that it would steal your sister's memories. A simple incantation, for me. She will not bother me or the children, at least, once you are gone.

There is one last remedy I could administer, after your death. I could try to bring you back. But it is not a thing lightly done. The risk is too great, and the children need me. In this last way, I have failed you again.

This morning the children came to say good-bye to you. Little Oliver, as always, was dutiful. Edmond is still too young to understand, but was very sweet. I tried to rouse you, to no avail. It seems your mind may already be at peace, with your body and soul soon to follow.

Rest, my love. Rest and wait. Our bond will never untether, even after death. All that separates us is time.

Dearly,
Your loving wife

Holly put the letter down. She tried to piece its contents together with what she already knew. The talk of potions and incantations confirmed that *It* was a witch. But she had written about Oliver as if he were dying. He must have gotten better. Or maybe she did bring him back, after all. And Edmond was her son. That would mean he was hundreds of years old. But he was still a child. And he had a brother. Little Oliver. What had happened to him? What had happened to them all?

Holly's thoughts were interrupted by a slow creaking sound. She turned. The bookcase on the far side of the room had moved. It was opening. She hoped, for a moment, that somehow it was Hector. But no.

On the other side was *It*.

The woman's back was hunched, as if she was in pain. When she stepped fully into the bedroom, though, and her red eyes rested on Holly, she straightened, coming to life. Holly searched her face for a hint of the humanity she had possessed in the letter, but it was gone.

It came around the bed, standing between Holly and the window. There was nowhere for her to run. She was trapped.

Holly reached behind her, grasping the pitcher that rested on the nightstand. She flung it at the woman as hard as she could.

The pitcher struck *It* on the forehead with a solid thud, then clattered down, breaking into pieces. She dropped to her knees. She put a hand to her face where she'd been hit. Blood seeped between her fingers, dripping to the floor.

The woman rose. The placid expression was gone from her face. As if channeling her inner wolf, she bared her teeth.

Holly reached for the washbasin, the only weapon she had left. She picked it up with two hands, twisting her waist like she was hurling a discus, and launched the bowl at the witch.

It ducked.

The bowl sailed right past her, striking the window.

The window cracked. One long fracture began to spread, to splinter, branching out across the glass. It shattered.

The witch came at Holly. From behind her came the fog. It poured through the broken window, washing over the woman, over Holly. It quickly filled the room, pulling them both deep into the past.

31

HOLLY WAS OUTSIDE. SHE WAS IN A COURTYARD BEHIND THE MANOR. A large, perfectly manicured green lawn stretched before her. She saw a series of square garden beds blooming with red and yellow flowers, and two perfectly symmetrical, rectangular hedges facing each other. Between the hedges, in the center of the yard, was a large circular fountain.

The woman in black stood next to her.

Holly's instinct was to run, to escape, to get as far from her as possible. But the woman in black hadn't moved. Wind blew her hair back, and her black dress flapped in the breeze, clinging to her legs.

She slowly turned to Holly. Her eyes were no longer red. They were brown.

"You're not him," she said.

Then she looked away from Holly, dismissing her. All of the woman's attention was on the fountain.

Two children were there. Both were dressed in old-fashioned clothes. One had brown hair. The other had blond hair and bright blue eyes.

It was Edmond.

Holly looked at *It*, who was transfixed by the scene before them. Holly realized that, just as she had seen her own past with Marco and Max and Hector, she was now seeing the witch's past.

"The Hiddenseek!" Edmond pulled at the other boy's white shirt. "You *promised*. You promised you'd play with me!"

"Yes, yes, fine," the other boy said. He did not sound very enthusiastic about it.

"Can we ask the Smith children to join us? Or James?" Edmond asked eagerly. "It's so much more fun with others."

"Later," the other boy said tersely. Edmond began to protest, but the other boy stopped him. "I *promise*. I will find others to join us. You go hide first."

"You have to count," Edmond said.

The other boy rolled his eyes. "One . . . two . . ."

Edmond jumped with excitement. He ran off, out of the courtyard and into the woods beyond.

The other boy stopped counting as he watched Edmond go. Then he walked to the house, opened the back door, and went inside.

At a nearby window, Holly saw a figure peering out. A woman with raven-black hair. She was the witch. A past version of her. But she was different. Her hair was immaculately curled and braided. Her dress was white and embroidered with flowers. Something shiny glinted at her neck.

Suddenly, the fog rushed in again. It didn't creep and surround them, like before, but instead washed over them, giving no chance for escape. It flowed over the fountain, over Holly, over everything.

When it cleared, Holly was no longer outside. She was inside a dark and moist cave. There was a shallow pool of water near the back. The woman in black was again beside her.

The past version of Edmond entered the grotto. He checked behind him to see if he was being followed, then tiptoed over to the pool of water. A few feet above it, on the wall of the cave, was a small alcove.

A perfect hiding spot.

Edmond sat at the edge of the pool. He whistled absentmindedly as he removed his shoes. It was a languid, melancholy tune. The same one, Holly realized, she had heard in the graveyard, the song that had lured *It* away.

With bare feet, Edmond waded in, sloshing through the water. He got to the other side, just below the alcove, and reached up, grasping the rocky surface of the cave wall. He climbed, his feet dripping, making tiny splashes in the water below.

He brought a knee up, trying to find a nook to rest his

foot. The rocks, though, were smooth and slippery. His feet couldn't find purchase, couldn't hold, and then he was dangling. His hands clung to a small, shallow groove in the wall, but they slid, down to his knuckles, down to his fingertips, and then to nothing.

Edmond fell.

His head hit the bottom of the shallow pool. His face dipped below the water. He didn't move.

The woman in black rushed to him and fell to her knees. She tried to lift him, but her hands passed right through him. He was nothing but a ghost. A figment. A memory. She couldn't help him or hold him. She couldn't even touch him. She could only watch it all unfold, powerless to change what had happened.

The witch huddled over Edmond's lifeless body. Holly didn't dare disturb her, and they stayed like that, alone together inside the woman's grief, until a frantic shout broke the silence.

"Edmond!" a voice called from behind. A woman's voice. "Which way, Oliver? Where is he?"

"Check in here," came the answer. "He sometimes hides in here."

The woman in white and the brown-haired boy entered the grotto. She stopped short at the cave opening as her eyes adjusted to the dark and she saw the figure of Edmond lying in the pool.

Her scream shattered the air.

She ran to Edmond. She got on her knees and lifted his head onto her lap. She sat in almost the exact same spot as the woman in black. Their two figures overlapped, ghostly mirrors of each other.

"Edmond?" the brown-haired boy said. He sounded terrified.

The woman in white screamed until she ran out of breath. What had begun as a shriek became a desperate, yearning wail, until finally collapsing and dying as an empty, whispering moan. It was the sound of the woman's heart escaping her body, breaking in two.

Her body slumped, drained of all strength. She swayed as if she were sleepwalking, or in a trance. She cradled Edmond in her arms, trembling.

Then she stopped. A calm passed over her. Slowly, she brought her head up. She sat upright, her posture unnaturally, painfully stiff. She stayed in that position, motionless, never taking a single breath, until, at last, she spoke.

"It's not too late."

She was suddenly filled with frantic energy and purpose. She leaned across Edmond's body, casting her hands about on the ground, patting, scratching, searching. "I need something sharp . . ." she whispered.

The brown-haired boy stepped toward the woman. "Mother?" he said, his voice fragile and desperate.

She spun to face him. Her eyes were bloodshot from tears. She hissed her response in a dry rasp, as if her throat were on fire.

"It's . . . not . . . too . . . late."

Her hand went to her chest, where a silver pendant hung below her neck. It was in the shape of a raven in flight, its arched, open wings ending in points as sharp as knives. She grasped the raven and pulled, snapping the thin chain.

She opened her palm. With the other hand she sliced, swiftly drawing the raven's silver wings across the tender skin below her fingers. A thin, bright red line formed, then flowed. In moments her hand was covered in blood.

She smeared the blood on her fingers and began tracing symbols on the rocky ground. Then she started to mutter, rhythmically, like a chant, coughing and snarling in a strange tongue.

Her head snapped back. Something like smoke, like fog, came from her mouth. It curled, drifting from her to Edmond. The fog took him up, cradled him.

He breathed it in.

Edmond's eyes popped open. They were gray. He cocked his neck and screamed.

Dark fog poured from his mouth. It gathered and swirled around him. It surrounded the brown-haired boy. It pummeled the woman in white. It seeped into her skin, her clothes. Her white dress turned black.

She covered her face with her hands. She screamed

again, this time in terror. Fog shot from her eyes, like steam spewing from a kettle. It spilled from her, filling the cave and beyond, leaving dark, empty holes where her eyes once were. Holes that slowly began to burn red.

Then the woman wavered, like her body was a reflection in the water. The same happened to Edmond and the brown-haired boy. They all became like smoke, like mist, and melted away. The memory was ending.

The woman in black, whose past they had just witnessed, was still there, on her knees. She turned around, facing Holly.

"You're not him," she said.

They were surrounded by thick fog now. Holly could no longer see the walls of the grotto, or the entrance.

Nearby, a hole in the fog opened. The woman took no notice.

Holly didn't hesitate. She ran, leaving the witch and all her haunted memories behind.

32

"WHERE'S HOLLY?" HECTOR ASKED AS HE FOLLOWED EDMOND farther into the woods.

They had rushed out of the manor, passing through a courtyard, past a fountain.

"Isn't that the way home?" Hector had asked. But Edmond told him they had to keep going. That Holly was in trouble.

"Just a bit farther," Edmond said.

Hector guessed Holly must have found a way out of the house. He hoped so. He couldn't believe how stupid he was for arguing with her before, for saying those things. Like any of that mattered right now.

When I find her, Hector promised himself, *the first thing I'm going to say is* I'm sorry.

The woods thickened, with branches hanging overhead like knobby, crooked fingers. Hector heard the sound of running water. They came across a creek, its shallow water trickling over a bed of rocks. They followed the creek until it brought them to a cave.

"In here," Edmond said to Hector. Drips of water echoed from inside.

They entered. The stream they had followed ended in a pool of water. Edmond pointed above the pool. There was a crevice there, like a little shelf. A hiding place.

"There," Edmond said. "Holly's back there."

Hector craned his neck. It didn't *look* like Holly was back there. "Where?"

"You can't see," Edmond said. "It's dark. But she hid in there. I think she might be hurt."

"OK," Hector said. "How do I get up there?"

"Take your shoes off," Edmond said. "Climb."

Hector sat on the rocks and started pulling off his shoes. "And you'll show us the way home? After I get her?"

"Of course." Edmond smiled. "We can do whatever you want. After."

Hector waded into the water. It was cold, and pebbles poked at his feet from the silty bottom. He got to the wall below the hiding spot and put his hands on the rock. It was wet and slippery.

"Go ahead," Edmond said. "Climb."

Hector reached and grabbed a rock jutting out from the wall. He pulled himself up but slipped back down. This would be tricky. He outstretched his arm and found another notch to hold on to. He lifted himself, finding a foothold on a little rock ledge. He made sure his hands were secure, then lifted a leg, placing his bare foot on a wide piece of slick stone. He put his weight on that foot and pushed himself higher, feeling along the rock for somewhere to grip.

But then his foot slipped.

Hector tried to hold on, but there was nothing to grab on to.

He fell. His body hit the water below with a splash.

And everything went black.

33

HOLLY WAS BACK IN THE BEDROOM. AS SOON AS SHE STEPPED from the fog, it retreated out the window, as if it was being inhaled by something outside. In moments, there was no trace of any mist, inside or out. Sunlight now peeked through the window, glinting on the broken glass.

Holly's thoughts reeled from all she had just seen.

The woman in white was the witch.

Edmond was her son.

He died playing hide-and-seek.

She tried to bring him back.

It went horribly wrong.

Edmond's parting words shot through her. *He is going to be just like me.* That's what he had said about Hector, before locking her in the bedroom.

The doorknob rattled. There was a *click*. The door opened.

A familiar face stepped into the room. A man with a wild mane of unkempt brown hair and a thick, bristly mustache obscuring his lips. He slumped like an invisible weight hung from his neck.

Oliver.

"You." He scowled at Holly. Then he noticed the broken window and the secret passage, still open in the wall. "What happened in here? Where is Edmond?"

"That's what I was going to ask you, Oliver," Holly said. "Or should I say *little* Oliver?"

He loomed over Holly. It reminded her too much of the way he had come for her when they first met.

"What did you say?" he demanded. "What did you call me?"

"Little Oliver," she said again. "That's what your mother called you, isn't it?"

It was a hunch she had from the letter she'd read and the memories she'd just seen. The witch's husband, Oliver, had, in fact, died. This Oliver was the brown-haired boy from the memories, the older son, named after his father. Somehow, he had aged, even though Edmond and the witch hadn't, but he was the same boy. He had to be.

"How do you know that?" He looked confused and angry. And there was something else Holly thought she saw cross his face. Shame.

"She's your mother," Holly said. "Yours *and* Edmond's. Isn't she?"

Oliver didn't answer. He deflated. His body sagged. He went to the edge of the bed and sat, hunching over, his elbows resting on his knees.

"Yes," he said. "Edmond is my brother."

For a moment, Holly almost felt bad for him.

"What happened?" she asked. "What is this place? Why did you bring me here?"

"Why?" Oliver laughed bitterly. "Because it's my fault he was lost. And I have never stopped paying the price."

He rose, walking over to the broken pitcher on the floor. He knelt.

"My mother tried to bring him back," he said. "She failed. So we were trapped in time. Like in a memory. Edmond's last memory." He shook his head and gave a small, sad smile. "In his favorite game. *The Hiddenseek*."

"But why take us?" Holly needed to know. She had to know why she had older brothers she couldn't remember, why she'd probably never see her parents again, why her entire life had been turned inside out.

"Because I told Edmond I would play with him. It's what he remembered. So here we are. I'm cursed to fulfill my last promise to him. Over and over. Forever."

"You have to find others to play," Holly whispered.

He nodded. "Edmond doesn't age. I grow older, but only when I enter your world. Those few brief minutes each time . . ."

Oliver rubbed his finger on the floor. He held it up for

Holly to see. It was dipped in blood, from when Holly had thrown the pitcher at the witch.

"Tell me," he said. "How do you know all of this? What happened in here?"

"I was pulled into the fog." Holly motioned toward the window. "With your mother."

Oliver looked grim.

"Help me find my brother," she pleaded, but he wouldn't meet her eyes. "Please, you have to help me."

"No," Oliver said. "I don't. He is your concern, not mine." Oliver turned as if to go.

"But Hector is *with* Edmond," she called to him.

Oliver stopped. At last, he met Holly's gaze. He looked surprised.

"Edmond said he was going to make Hector *just like him*," Holly explained. "What does that mean?"

Oliver looked alarmed at first. "He wouldn't . . ." he said, but then he quickly shook his head, banishing whatever thought he had. "He just wants someone who will play with him."

"No!" Holly grabbed his arm, trying to force him to react, to care. "Don't you get it? Edmond doesn't really want Hector. He wants someone who will *always* be there to play with him. He wants a *brother*. He wants *you!*"

Oliver shook his head. "It's not *me* he wants." He turned his back on Holly. "He wants what I should have been."

"Please—"

"Go save your brother, if you can," Oliver said. He walked to the window and stared out of it. "There is no saving mine."

Holly backed out the door, leaving. There was no use. He wasn't going to help.

She raced down the stairs. The house was quiet, but she could just make out the faint trill of birdsong and leaves whispering in the wind—the subtle sounds of the outdoors. A door was open somewhere. She found it just around the other side of the staircase. It led to the courtyard.

It was like stepping into ancient ruins. Holly had seen this same courtyard in the witch's memory, tidy and neatly trimmed. Now wild grass and weeds overran the garden beds. The hedges were overgrown.

At the center of the yard was the fountain. A girl with rainbow hair sat on the edge.

"Petunia!" Holly ran to her.

Petunia looked. Her face lit up. She leapt off the fountain and grabbed Holly in a fierce hug.

"Holly!" she gasped. "You're all right!"

"Where's George?" Holly asked. "Have you seen Hector?"

"George . . . didn't make it." Petunia looked back toward the house, frowning. "He saved me."

Holly bit her lip. She swallowed an ache at the back of her throat. What more could possibly happen? How much more would this terrible place take?

"I saw Oliver," Petunia said. She thumbed toward the fountain. "He said Edmond was right. This really is the way home. It's *home base,* you could say."

Holly peered inside the fountain. It was filled with swirling fog instead of water.

"Why are you still here, then?" Holly asked. "You could have left."

Petunia shook her head. "No, I couldn't." She punched Holly lightly on the arm. "Not without my friends."

Despite everything, a smile broke across Holly's face. She hadn't known how much she needed to hear those words. Not until Petunia said them.

"Friends," Holly said. "I could really use one of those."

A pale hand emerged from the fog and grasped the edge of the fountain.

"Petunia," Holly whispered, taking a step back. "Petunia, move!"

But it was too late.

A head rose from the mist. An ivory face with hair as black as midnight. With eyes red like a dying sun. *It* pulled herself up, as if climbing from the depths of the earth.

She placed a hand on the back of Petunia's head. Petunia had just enough time to look surprised before turning to stone.

The woman in black tumbled out of the fountain, falling to the grass. She moaned. She clawed at the ground. She grasped handfuls of dirt. She crawled toward Holly.

Holly wanted to scream in shock and pain and rage, but the sound died in her throat. There was no point. *It* was never going to give up, The witch would keep coming for her. She would never stop.

"Why?" Holly finally managed to croak. "Why are you doing this? What do you *want* from us?"

You're not him.

That was what the woman had said to Holly when they were in the memory.

It's not us she wants, Holly realized. It was Edmond. *It* wanted *Edmond.*

And suddenly Holly knew what she had to do.

34

HOLLY SPRINTED AWAY FROM THE WOMAN, FROM THE FOUNTAIN, and into the woods. She had a sense of what she was looking for. In the witch's memory, she'd seen the path Edmond had taken to the cave, all those years ago.

She broke out of a copse of bushes and planted a foot directly in a shallow stream. Water soaked her shoe. She ran in the creek, splashing her way forward.

It ended at the grotto, which looked just as it had in the memory. Holly rushed inside.

The first thing she saw was Edmond. He was standing in a shallow pool, the water just covering his ankles.

Lying next to him, facedown in the water, was Hector.

"Hector!" Holly screamed.

She ran to him. She knelt, water seeping into her clothes. She put her hand under his head, lifting his face out of the water. It was pale. She cradled his limp body in her arms.

"No," she cried. "No."

"It's OK," Edmond said. "She'll bring him back. Then we can play some more."

Edmond was delusional. He thought his mother was going to use her spell, her curse, whatever it was, to bring Hector back to life?

But Hector was gone.

"What is *wrong* with you?" Holly sobbed.

"She'll bring him back," Edmond said again.

"No, she won't." Holly held Hector to her. "She doesn't care about him. Can't you see that? The only thing she wants is *you*."

Edmond stared blankly at her.

Holly felt her chest go numb and hollow. Grief was taking over. She let it.

She closed her eyes. For the first time since the beginning, she stopped longing for home. What was the point of going home now, without Hector? Would her parents even remember him? Even worse, would she forget Hector too?

No. This place had taken him. She wouldn't let it take her memory of him too. She wouldn't let it have that.

Holly reached for memories of Hector, holding them as closely as she held his body. She remembered the easy way he laughed and made friends. His boneheaded way of charging into things without thinking. Even their fights. She held on to those too. He knew just how to hurt her, because nobody else in the world knew her so well.

She squeezed him even tighter. She wouldn't let him go. She would never let go.

"Aghh." Hector's body convulsed.

Holly felt water spew onto her back.

"Holly," he coughed, his voice clenched and weak. "Holly, you're crushing me."

Holly opened her eyes. Hector was staring back at her. He looked confused.

He looked *alive*.

She couldn't believe it. He was OK.

"I'm sorry!" Hector blurted out. He sat up, pulling himself away from Holly's grasp but keeping a hand on her arm. "I swore if I ever saw you again I'd say I'm sorry. I shouldn't have said those things and—"

Then his jaw dropped open. His eyes bulged. He looked scared.

"What?" Holly asked. "What is it?"

She felt a hand on her head.

It spread fast. She could feel her neck stiffen. Then her torso, then her arms and legs. She couldn't move her fingers or toes. She couldn't feel the clothes on her skin or her heart beating in her chest. Her nose twitched, one final time, then went still.

The last thing she saw was Hector reaching for her. His face was shocked and terrified. The last thing she heard was him calling her name. He was going to be so sad. She couldn't leave him in that much anguish. She had to do something, anything to ease his pain.

She pulled reserves of strength from deep within, strength she didn't know she had. Her face was already hard and solid, but she fought against it. She pushed and pushed until, at last, for one brief moment, her heart proved stronger than stone. She moved, just a little, just the corners of her mouth. She hoped it was enough. She hoped he understood.

He was alive. She loved him. That was all that mattered.

There are countless statues scattered all throughout the Hiddenseek.

Only one has a smile.

35

HECTOR BURIED HIS FACE IN HIS HANDS. HOLLY WAS A STATUE. She was a statue, and it was all his fault. He would never forgive himself. Worse, he knew that Holly had, in fact, forgiven *him*. Of course she had. It was the right thing to do, and she always did what was right.

It crumpled up on the floor of the cave. Edmond backed away from her. Hector knew he should probably run, that she would get up soon and turn him to stone too. But none of that mattered to him anymore. He just wanted this all to be over with.

"Why did you take me here?" he shouted at Edmond. "Why *her*? It shouldn't have been *her*. It should have been *you*. This is all *your* fault!"

Edmond didn't say anything. He leaned against the wall of the grotto, looking lost and confused.

"Edmond," said a deep voice from the cave entrance.

It was the strange man who had brought them here.

Oliver. He ducked into the grotto, reaching out to Edmond with an open hand.

"Olly," Edmond whispered. "Olly-Olly oxen-free."

"That's right," Oliver said. His voice was measured, like he was trying to keep Edmond calm. "You have to come with me now. She'll be up soon."

"No," Hector said. He got in front of Oliver, blocking him from Edmond. "Let her get him. He deserves it!" Tears rolled down Hector's face. He knew he was lashing out, that he wasn't thinking straight. He didn't care.

Oliver grabbed Hector by the shoulders and moved him out of the way.

"Do you think I would allow that to happen?" he said. "After all these years? Do you think I would lose him *again*?" Oliver's face began to warm with anger. "How do you think he's survived this long? *I* am the one who protects him. *I* am the one who follows him. *I* am the one who draws her away."

"I don't care!" Hector shouted. "I want my sister back!"

"AND I WANT MY BROTHER!" Oliver's eyes welled. His furious voice quivered, mixing with anguish.

"Olly?" Edmond came up behind his brother. He wrapped his small hand around Oliver's larger one.

It was still on the ground. Her red eyes were fixed on Edmond and Oliver. She wriggled forward, struggling to reach them.

"I'm scared," Edmond said. "But I think I can do it."

"Do what?" Oliver asked. "What are you talking about?"

"I can go to her," Edmond answered.

"No." Oliver got on his knees. "You can still play. That's what you want, right?"

"I thought so," Edmond said. He looked at the statue of Holly, then to the woman in black. "But now I think . . . she needs me."

"I don't know what will happen," Oliver said. "If I let her catch you. You might not come back."

"What if you come with me?" Edmond asked. "Will you? Will you come with me? Then we can play whatever *you* want." He smiled hopefully. "I *promise.*"

Oliver closed his eyes. He took a deep breath, his chest swelling. Then he let it go.

"Of course," he said. "We'll go. Together."

Edmond and Oliver walked hand in hand toward the woman in black. She pulled herself up onto her knees. She opened her arms and took them in.

Oliver turned into a statue first, his hair solidifying into intricate curls of stone. Next was Edmond, his eyes closed, a look of peace etched on his face.

And last was the woman in black. The darkness melted off her, running like ink, revealing a dress of purest white. The red light in her eyes dimmed and blinked out, revealing human eyes overflowing with relief.

The gray stone began forming at her feet, inching up, covering her legs, her waist. She clutched her children close, holding them as her arms stiffened. She bent her head, her sons clasped to her in a never-ending embrace.

Hector was all alone. He could hear the sounds of forest creatures stirring outside, the wind brushing the trees.

He was the last one left in the Hiddenseek. He had no idea what to do next.

What would Holly do? Hector wondered how long he'd be asking himself that. Probably forever. *Holly would find the way home. She'd never give up until she found it. That's what she would do.*

Hector would try. He'd go look for the way home. But first he had to do one last thing.

He waded back into the water and took his sister's hand. Her fingers were coarse and petrified, but oddly they felt warm. There was so much he wanted to say, but words didn't seem like enough. He couldn't possibly say everything he was feeling, how much he would miss her, how much regret he had.

"Good-bye, Holly." He leaned his head against hers and squeezed her hand one final time.

Her hand squeezed back.

Their hands clasped, their fingers locking together. Color and life returned to Holly's body, spreading like sunlight breaking over the horizon. Soon the last of the gray drained away. The hint of a smile on her face never wavered, though. A spark of joy had settled deep inside her and wouldn't be moved.

"Hey," she said. "Let's go home."

36

HOLLY LED HECTOR OUT OF THE CAVE. THE GROUND WAS WET. The sun was out, but there was a light drizzle. Raindrops dripped from the ends of leaves, plunking softly on the grass.

They made their way back through the woods. When they came to the edge of the trees, someone came running to them from the courtyard, her pink and blue hair shimmering in the light.

"Holly! Hector!" Petunia wrapped them in an embrace so fierce she almost brought them to the ground.

"Petunia!" Holly said. "You're OK!"

Petunia grinned, bobbing her head up and down in a yes.

Someone came out the back door of the manor house. It was George.

"George!" Holly called to him. He saw them and waved, and they all ran to meet one another at the fountain.

"What happened?" George asked. "How am I not a statue anymore?"

"Long story short?" Holly smiled. "*It* found what she was looking for."

They all peered into the fountain. The fog was even more agitated, spinning and churning as if inside a blender.

Then the fog rose. It swirled out of the fountain like a cyclone. It expanded, growing wider and wider.

"What's happening?" Hector backed away.

"It's OK." Holly grabbed his hand.

The fog spread out, curling around them. The fountain, the hedges, even the manor, all became blurry, wavering like a mirage. Everything before them began to dissipate, drifting away, piece by piece.

"What was it like?" Hector asked. He had to raise his voice to be heard over the sudden rush of wind.

"What was what like?" Holly replied.

"Being a statue."

"Oh," she said. "Like nothing. Like being asleep. Why do you ask?"

He shrugged. "Just wondering. You realize I'm the only one who *didn't* get caught. You know what that means, right?"

"No," Holly said. "What does that mean?"

Hector smiled. "I won."

They laughed.

The fog filled Holly's vision until it was all she could

see. She felt as if she were caught in the eye of the storm. Images whirled and flashed in front of her eyes. For a moment, she thought she could still see the forest. It was hazy, like a memory, like a dream. Three figures ran through the trees. A mother with black hair and a light, musical laugh. Two little boys, one with blond hair, one with brown. They were playing a game, all their cares forgotten, lost in their own world.

EPILOGUE

"YOU GUYS REALLY WANT TO PLAY THIS?" MOM HELD THE board game box in her hand. *"Memory?"*

Marco smirked. "An inside joke. But yeah, let's play."

They gathered around the coffee table in the living room. Max had an arm down to his elbow in a bag of chips. Hector was doodling on a piece of paper, killing time until they started. Dad was in the kitchen finishing the dishes.

"I go first!" Dad yelled from the sink. "Oldest always goes first!"

Holly's phone vibrated. Someone had sent another message on the group text.

Petunia: Movie?

Holly quickly texted back.

Holly: Can't. Family night.

George: Don't let Hector cheat!

Petunia: Have fun! How about tomorrow?
Everyone in?

Holly: Yes!

George: Bring your brothers!

"Holly," Mom said. "Put your phone away. You can talk to your friends later."

Holly tucked it in her pocket. Dad came in and took a seat on the floor. Mom slid the top off the box and started setting everything up.

Hector scooted over, and Holly sat down next to him. She looked to see what he was drawing. It was a half-formed object. Maybe a leg. Maybe the wing of an airplane.

"What're you drawing?" she asked.

"Don't know yet," he said. "It's your turn."

He held the pencil out to her. She smiled and took it.

This was still her favorite game.

ACKNOWLEDGMENTS

THE JOURNEY TO BRING *THE HIDDENSEEK* OUT OF HIDING and into the world has been one of the most worthwhile and rewarding experiences a writer could hope for, and it wouldn't have happened without the talent, guidance, support, and love of an amazing group of people.

Enormous thanks to Jen Klonsky and the team at Putnam, and especially to my brilliant editor, Stephanie Pitts, who always believed in me and in this book and who did so much to bring out my best. Huge thanks also to Matt Phipps and to cover artist Pete Lloyd for his extraordinary and iconic work.

An infinite number of thank-yous to Sara Shandler, Joelle Hobeika, and Josh Bank for taking a chance on me and for giving me so much encouragement and support, and to Les Morgenstein and everyone at Alloy for working so hard to bring this book to life.

None of this happens without real-life superhero David Yoon. Thanks for being there for me at every step. Thanks also to Nicola Yoon, who said, "Write it as a book, dummy" (right on both counts!), and to all my friends and family who kindly read the early drafts.

Thank you, Mom and Dad, for never doubting I could do it and for never saying no when I asked for a book. Thanks to my brothers, Aaron and David, for putting the real magic in all our games.

Thanks to my uncle Rick Giusti for the books that made me want to write. Thanks to Nick Almaraz for being the sounding board for every idea.

To Lucia and Tommy, thank you for the joy and inspiration every day. And to Jessica—having you by my side, year after year, draft after draft, has been and will always be the best part of this. I can't wait to share with you whatever comes next.

ABOUT THE AUTHOR

Austin Pro Photo

NATE CERNOSEK lives in Austin, Texas, with his wife and two children. *The Hiddenseek* is his first novel.